SWARM
CODE NAME FIRESTORM

STRIPES PUBLISHING
An imprint of Little Tiger Press
1 The Coda Centre, 189 Munster Road,
London SW6 6AW

A paperback original
First published in Great Britain in 2015

Text copyright © Simon Cheshire, 2015
Cover illustration copyright © Peter Minister, 2015
Cover background and inside imagery courtesy of www.shutterstock.com

ISBN: 978-1-84715-451-4

A CIP catalogue record for this book is available
from the British Library.

Printed and bound in the UK.

10 9 8 7 6 5 4 3 2 1

SWARM

CODE NAME FIRESTORM

SIMON CHESHIRE

Stripes

SWARM

DEPARTMENT OF MICRO-ROBOTIC INTELLIGENCE

SPECIALISTS IN NANOTECHNOLOGY AND BIOMIMICRY

HEAD OF DEPARTMENT

Beatrice Maynard: Code name QUEEN BEE

HUMAN OPERATIVES

Prof. Thomas Miller: TECHNICIAN
Alfred Berners: PROGRAMMER
Simon Turing: DATA ANALYST

SWARM OPERATIVES

WIDOW

DIVISION: Spider
LENGTH: 1.5 cm
WEIGHT: 1 gram
FEATURES:

- 360° vision and recording function
- Produces silk threads and webs stronger than steel
- Extremely venomous bite
- Can walk on any surface – horizontal, vertical or upside down

CHOPPER

DIVISION: Dragonfly
LENGTH: 12 cm
WEIGHT: 0.8 grams
FEATURES:

- Telescopic vision with zoom, scanning and recording functions
- Night vision and thermal imaging abilities
- High-speed flight with super control and rapid directional change

NERO

DIVISION: Scorpion
LENGTH: 12 cm
WEIGHT: 30 grams
FEATURES:
- Strong, impact-resistant exoskeleton
- Pincers to grab and hold, with high dexterity
- Venomous sting in tail
- Capable of high-speed attack movements

SABRE

DIVISION: Mosquito
LENGTH: 2 cm
WEIGHT: 2.5 milligrams
FEATURES:
- Long proboscis (mouthparts) for extracting DNA and injecting tracking technology and liquids to cause paralysis or memory loss
- Specialist in stealth movement without detection
- Capable of recording low frequency, low-volume sound

HERCULES

DIVISION: Stag beetle
LENGTH: 5 cm
WEIGHT: 50 grams
FEATURES:
- Extra-tough membrane on wing shells to withstand extreme force and pressure
- Serrated claw for sawing through any material
- Can lay surveillance 'eggs' for tracking and data analysis

MORPH

DIVISION: Centipede
LENGTH: 5 cm (10 cm when fully extended)
WEIGHT: 100 milligrams
FEATURES:
- Flexible, gelatinous body with super-strong grip
- Ability to dig and burrow
- Laser-mapping sensory functions

SIRENA

DIVISION: Butterfly
LENGTH: 7 cm
WEIGHT: 0.3 grams
FEATURES:
- Uses beauty rather than stealth for protection
- Expert in reconnaissance missions – can gather environmental data through high-sensitivity antennae

CHAPTER ONE

Thursday 2:00 p.m.

At first glance, the man walking down Queen Victoria Street, in the heart of the City of London, looked no different to anyone else. He was a tall man, with neatly cut hair and an unremarkable face. He wore a black overcoat and carried a briefcase.

Nobody paid him any attention. If they had, they might have seen that his eyes were glazed and unfocused, as if he was awake and asleep at the same time.

SWARM

He walked slowly, his briefcase swinging gently in his hand. He arrived at a large road junction and crossed a paved area where a statue of a horse and rider looked down on the busy scene below.

Without changing his pace, he pulled a flat black electronic device, about the size of a smartphone, from the pocket of his coat. He placed it against the side of his head. Tiny suckers shot out of it and attached the machine tightly against his temple. Small lights along its side flashed and it began to emit a series of beeps and tones.

The man stopped, put down his briefcase and shrugged off his overcoat, letting it drop to the ground. Then he swung the briefcase over his shoulder. As it moved, metal wires snaked out and whipped around him, transforming it into a kind of backpack. Panels on the back of it slid open, revealing a mass of circuits.

Next, the device attached to the man's head opened. It slid a narrow visor across his eyes, masking them with shifting green digital displays.

By now, the man was getting funny looks from

passers-by. He didn't take any notice of them. He crossed the road, his stride never changing, and entered the huge stone building that was the headquarters of the National Deposit and Finance Bank.

Inside, there was an enormous hall with a polished marble floor and a high, vaulted ceiling. Customers queued at cashier desks. Staff bustled here and there.

The moment the man strode in, he raised his arm. Dozens of tiny heat-seeking darts instantly fired from a tube hidden in the sleeve of his shirt. They spread out, moving at lightning speed. All the customers and most of the staff were hit within 1.7 seconds. They crumpled to the floor, unconscious.

The remaining staff, protected behind bulletproof screens, reached for the alarm buttons beside their desks. But before any alarm was pressed, the man's backpack sent out a jagged arc of electricity. It hit the screens and they shattered with a deafening crash. The staff screamed and ducked. A second buzzing arc hit the alarm buttons and fried them until nothing remained but smoking wires. The overload surged on through the building's electrical systems and burned them out.

The man stopped and turned. 4.9 seconds had passed since he walked in.

OBJECTIVE 1: DISABLE STAFF AND
SECURITY - ACHIEVED
OBJECTIVE 2: PREVENT INTERFERENCE -
BEGIN

He reached round and drew a bulbous, gun-like object from his backpack. He fired it and a large green ball shot out towards the twin glass doors through which he'd arrived. The ball splattered right in the centre, where the two doors met, then instantly set into a hard seal, preventing anyone else from entering the bank.

The man turned back. Crunching over what remained of the bulletproof screens, he headed for the vault at the far end of the hall.

The staff who'd been behind the screens were now cowering in a corner. One of them reached for her phone with trembling fingers. The movement was detected by the man's backpack and it beeped. Without breaking step, he swung round and fired another green glob at the phone. It was knocked to the floor and encased in a rock-hard shell, completely useless.

The shining steel door to the vault was large and round. To one side was a single massive hinge. On the other was the locking wheel and entry coder that controlled access.

The target sights on the man's visor glowed, zooming in on the vault. He took a disc-like machine from his backpack and flung it towards the door as if it was a frisbee.

The magnetic disc clanged against the exact centre of the steel door. It began to spin, emitting a droning, howling sound, which grew louder and louder. The entire vault door started to shimmer, as sound vibrations pulsed through it. Suddenly, the metal buckled and burst and the door caved in, leaving shreds of metal around a gaping hole. The disc dropped to the floor and self-destructed in a ball of fire.

OBJECTIVE 3: TAKE ITEMS – BEGIN

The man stepped into the vault, taking care not to snag himself on the shredded steel. Inside were rows of safety deposit boxes set into the walls. He ignored them all and marched over to a series of metal crates clamped to the floor. He placed a thin device, no larger than a pencil, against the complex electronic lock on one of the crates. The lock suddenly flashed red, then deactivated, springing the crate's lid open. Inside, neatly stacked, were bars of solid gold.

Meanwhile, police cars had blocked off the area outside the entrance to the bank. Sirens whooped and people craned their necks from behind lines of yellow and black tape marked "Do Not Cross". A senior officer arrived and spoke to one of the constables gathered by the entrance.

"The doors are sealed?" he shouted. "With what?"

"We don't know, sir."

"Blow them apart!"

"We can't do that, sir," gulped the constable.

"It's a high-security bank. Those doors are built to withstand attack."

"Then find another way in."

"All the internal electrics are fried, sir. Security doors are on lockdown. We've got to bypass everything. We've got people working on it at the rear of the building, but it'll take a few minutes."

A woman in a smart business suit stood by, unnoticed. She smiled to herself. She was known only by her codename, Agent K, and she worked for a top-secret branch of the British secret service known as SWARM.

She spoke softly into the communicator tucked in her right ear. "Hive 2 to Hive 1, are you inside the bank?"

A calm, electronic voice answered her. "Affirmative."

At that moment, the micro-robotic SWARM operatives were crawling up out of the bank's staff toilet. They had been created using the most advanced technology in the world. Tough enough to survive extreme environments, packed with sensors and weapons, and programmed for high intelligence. They were a

team of undercover agents like no other.

There was a dragonfly, codenamed Chopper, coordinating their mission. Behind him came Nero, a scorpion, and Hercules, a stag beetle. After them came Sabre, a tiny mosquito, and a spider called Widow. Two more robots, Morph the centipede and Sirena the butterfly, were stationed outside the building.

"I'm glad we don't have a human's sense of smell," said Hercules, scanning the toilet cubicle they had emerged into.

"Or a human's size," said Nero. "The bank robber won't have planned for anyone getting in through the drainage system."

The robots had been activated and rushed to the scene after SWARM's advanced surveillance systems had intercepted police messages. Reports from one of London's most secure banks about an armed intruder were something that needed investigating.

"It's fortunate that our HQ is nearby," said Nero.

"Systems to attack mode," said Chopper calmly. "We don't know what we'll face out there."

"I'm live," answered the others.

The five micro-robots scurried and flew across the white floor tiles and through the narrow gap at the bottom of the toilet door. They emerged into a short corridor, which led to the bank's large main hall.

"Morph, anything to report?" signalled Chopper.

Morph the centipede had scuttled up the outside of the building, unseen, to a top corner of the main entrance where the police were positioned.

"My sensors show that the entrance has been sealed with a fast-setting organic polymer," he transmitted. "Its origin is unknown. I've sent the data back to HQ."

"Stay at your current location," said Chopper. "Keep watch."

"Logged," said Morph.

"Sirena?" signalled Chopper.

Sirena the butterfly was at the back of the building, fluttering a few metres above street level. She was keeping watch on the police officers who were trying to open the rear exits. "No change

here," she reported. "Deep scans confirm one attacker only. High levels of electronic activity. Humans inside are unharmed, but unconscious or in hiding."

"He must be armed with something highly destructive," said Morph.

The five robots inside the building made their move. Humans were in danger, so their mission priority was to stop the intruder as fast as possible.

They shot out into the main hall, dragonfly and mosquito buzzing high into the air, scorpion and beetle racing across the marble floor. The spider fired thin lines of web and swung herself in long, precise arcs.

The man in the vault was placing three heavy bars of gold into his backpack. That gold was worth around £600,000. It was all he'd been ordered to take, and all his backpack could carry.

He paused. Data streamed across the inside of his visor.

UNUSUAL MOVEMENT DETECTED!
REMOTE CONTROLLED CAMERAS?
DRONE WEAPONS?

CODE NAME FIRESTORM

PAUSE CURRENT OBJECTIVE

NEW OBJECTIVE: DESTROY

He stood up straight, spun on his heel and stepped out of the vault.

"He knows we're here," said Nero.

"How?" said Hercules. "Our systems are shielded."

Chopper's advanced eye-lenses zoomed in on the man. His circuits analyzed and calculated. "He has a motion-detection pod."

"To spot us, he must have technology above even military or secret-service specifications," said Hercules.

Suddenly a box-like section jutted forward from the man's backpack. It fired a miniature missile, which roared through the air towards Chopper and Sabre. The robots' advanced flight systems whipped them aside just in time and the missile hit the high ceiling. There was an almighty bang and a flash of flame. A shower of stone fragments burst across the hall and clouds of dust billowed down.

"Sabre! Nero!" signalled Chopper. "The dust will help mask our movements. Approach him

from opposite sides. Sting him!"

"I'm live," they both said, immediately racing towards the man.

Using the dust clouds as cover, Nero dashed over, while Sabre buzzed in a wide semi-circle. Sabre's needle-like mouthparts loaded up a pellet, ready to inject.

The man's backpack bleeped.

SMALL OBJECT AT FLOOR LEVEL

MINIATURE CAMERA OR SURVEILLANCE DEVICE SUSPECTED

NEW OBJECTIVE: DESTROY

As Nero shot forward, the man aimed a kick that sent the scorpion flying. Nero smacked into a nearby wall and dropped to the floor, upside down and motionless, his systems knocked into emergency shutdown.

"I'm going in," said Sabre.

"Wait," said Chopper. "It's too dangerous! He spotted Nero despite the dust and we can't have two agents down. Widow, distract him so Sabre can attack."

Instantly, the spider dived out of the dust cloud, zipping along a microscopic thread. Sure enough, the man's visor detected the movement. He swung round towards Widow. Sabre buzzed overhead.

The man twisted the barrel of his sealant-firing gun, adjusting its output. As Sabre dived from high above, aiming for the man's neck, the gun was struck against the ground, pointing upwards. Its barrel suddenly opened and fat balls of glue fired out in all directions. Electronic components inside the balls were instantly detected by the SWARM.

"Evasive manoeuvres!" said Chopper.

The glue-balls snaked at high speed through the air, homing in on the robots, following the tiny changes in air currents that they made as they moved. Even the SWARM couldn't move fast enough to avoid them. Sabre, barely three centimetres from his target, was hit first. The impact shot him across the room.

At last, Nero's systems rebooted and he flipped himself over. "No damage," he reported. Then a large ball of glue hit him squarely between his

pincers. He was stuck fast.

Chopper, Widow and Hercules suffered the same fate. Within two seconds, all five had been trapped by the glue.

The man took off his backpack. He operated a couple of switches inside and it emitted a series of beeps. Holding the backpack up, he aimed at the wall on the opposite side of the hall to the vault.

A set of three miniature missiles whirred into view. The man touched a sensor beside them. With a loud *whoosh*, all three launched at once and shot across the hall.

The impact made the entire building shake. A huge section of the wall exploded outwards and daylight burst in through the hole. Beyond, a section of the narrow street to the side of the bank was now visible and alarms, set off by the explosion, were sounding all around.

"That's his escape route," signalled Chopper. "Status report."

"Online, but unable to move," was the answer from Nero, Hercules, Widow and Sabre.

"The explosion is causing panic," transmitted

Morph at the front of the building. "The police are trying to calm down the public and work out what caused it."

"I'm closing in on the site of the explosion," said Sirena. "Large amounts of debris are on both sides of the road. Directly across from the bank, there's a set of steps leading to the Underground rail system."

"Plenty of places to hide or slip away," said Chopper. "That'll be where he's heading."

The man's visor retracted. He pulled the electronic device away from the side of his head, and dropped it into his backpack, alongside the gold bars. He now looked like an ordinary member of the public again, and the backpack had become a briefcase once more.

"Can anyone get free?" signalled Chopper.

"Negative," said Widow.

"Negative," said Nero. "My pincers are wedged, I can't cut through this stuff."

"Me neither," said Hercules. "My claw is completely covered."

Agent K's voice cut into the SWARM communications network. "Hive 2 to Hive 1.

I'm taking charge of the police operation. I've identified myself to them as a secret service agent. Can we proceed to intercept the attacker?"

The man brushed some of the dust off his shoulders, then marched steadily towards the hole in the wall.

"Negative," signalled Chopper. "He's still likely to be heavily armed. Leave this to the SWARM."

"OK," said Agent K, "but don't let him get away!"

The man was approaching the hole, his footsteps grating against the scattered fragments of stone and plaster on the floor. Within moments, he would be out in the open, across the road and down the steps.

"Should I tail him?" transmitted Sirena from outside. "If we let him think he's escaped, we might be able to capture him later."

"If he can detect and disable the five of us in here," said Nero, "he can do the same to you. We have to stop him immediately."

"My wings and legs are stuck," said Sabre, "but I can move my head. I could fire a sting at him?"

"Your mechanism isn't meant to function at a distance," said Chopper. "It's designed for injecting."

"I'll divert all power into it," said Sabre.

"Which might blow your head apart," said Hercules.

The man was less than five metres from the ragged hole.

"No time. Must take action!" In an instant, Sabre rerouted his energy cells. A buzz of power suddenly pulsed through his needle-like mouthparts. He took aim, his targeting systems struggling to cope with the massive energy surge. His sensors blinked and began to overload.

Two metres.

With a high-pitched hiss, a microscopic pellet shot from Sabre's proboscis.

It hit the man on the back of the neck. He jerked to a stop. For a moment, he tottered unsteadily, then tumbled backwards to the floor with a loud thud.

"Stinger delivered," said Sabre, his voice becoming a low slur from the strain on his systems.

"Good shot," said Nero.

Chopper signalled Agent K and seconds later she appeared at the hole in the wall. "I've told the police to keep back until I give them the all-clear. Quite a mess in here!"

Working fast, she began to free the SWARM robots, using a high-intensity laser beam hidden inside what looked like a pen to cut them free. All five were still encrusted with solidified glue. She placed them into a metal case, and put the case in her pocket.

"We'd better get you back to the lab as soon as possible," she said. She hurried over to the other end of the hall, where the bank employees were hiding under a couple of desks. She radioed the police outside. "OK, you've got a green light. Get the medics in here to check everyone. The attacker is mine."

The man Sabre had stung was beginning to regain his senses. Agent K took charge of his deadly briefcase weapon.

He rubbed his head, blinking sleepily. "Wh-where am I? Wh-what happened?"

"You're under arrest," said Agent K,

crouching down beside him.

"What?" cried the man in alarm. "Why? What have I done?"

Agent K frowned at him. "Don't try the memory-loss trick, I've seen it before."

Sirena had fluttered into the bank through the hole in the wall. She was now close to Agent K. Her electronic voice came over the SWARM network. "Voice stress levels indicate he's not lying," she said.

Agent K's eyes widened in surprise. "Who are you?" she asked the man.

"My name's Tim," he said nervously. "Tim Jones. I'm a primary school teacher. What am I doing here? The last thing I remember is leaving home this morning."

"Readings confirmed," said Sirena. "He really doesn't know what he's just done."

Agent K helped Mr Jones to his feet. He looked around the wrecked bank, scared and startled. A police officer trudged over to Agent K. He took no notice of the butterfly that was circling high above their heads.

"Have you seen what's in the vault?" he said.

"No," said Agent K. "You take Mr Jones here down to the station. He's all yours."

Picking up the briefcase, she crossed to the vault. Stepping carefully over the shards of metal, she went inside. Written in marker pen across the marble floor, in large capital letters, was a message:

THE FIRESTORM WILL RAGE

CHAPTER TWO

2:51 p.m.

"Ready?"

"Activate the control sphere, please, Alfred."

SWARM's resident Programmer, Alfred Berners, was older than the other members of the organization, with a shock of white hair and a heavily lined face. He was also one of the world's most brilliant computer scientists, and had designed the brains built into the SWARM micro-robots.

In the SWARM laboratory, deep beneath

the busy streets of central London, machines hummed and screens streamed data. Above one of the lab's long workbenches, a shiny transparent force field suddenly flickered into life.

"Thank you, Alfred," said Professor Miller. He was SWARM's senior technician, a stern-looking, bald-headed man in a white lab coat and glasses. He placed his hands above a bank of sensors built into the workbench, and inside the force field a set of mechanical hands flexed. They mirrored his movements exactly.

At the centre of the force field was the briefcase weapon Tim Jones has used during the bank raid. The professor was examining it under carefully controlled conditions.

"How are you getting on, Simon?" said Alfred Berners, turning to the third and final person present in the lab. This was Simon Turing, SWARM's brilliant Data Analyst.

Simon brushed back his brown hair and rubbed his chin. "I'm running through Chopper's recordings of the entire incident. Whoever made those gadgets and weapons is a genius. Even I'm jealous of technology like that!"

At that moment, their boss swept into the room. Beatrice Maynard, known by the micro-robotic team as Queen Bee, was in charge of all SWARM operations. Simon, Alfred and the professor all sat up straight as she approached the workbench.

"Good," she said. "I'm in time to see the briefcase being opened."

"I've got it inside a micro-sonic shield, Ms Maynard," said Professor Miller. "Just in case there are any nasty surprises. We've scanned it, but some of the electronics inside are designed to block signals, so better safe than sorry. This force field can contain anything short of a major explosion."

Queen Bee stood at the professor's shoulder. "Go ahead," she nodded.

As the professor manipulated the mechanical hands inside the force field, Queen Bee asked Simon for an update.

"Those gadgets must have been made by an independent manufacturer, something way off the market," he said. "There's nothing like them in any database, anywhere in the world."

Inside the force field, the mechanical hands gently took hold of the briefcase.

"And we're certain this Tim Jones knows nothing?" asked Queen Bee.

"Certain," said Simon Turing. "I've got Sirena monitoring him at the police station. They're holding him for questioning, but the police are baffled. So am I, to be honest! He must have been under some form of hypnotic control, but exactly how it was done is currently a mystery."

"Have you checked his background?" said Queen Bee.

"Everything from the moment of his birth to the moment of his arrest. He's exactly what he claims to be. He's a teacher, has been for fifteen years. He's never been in trouble with the police, he's never even had so much as a parking ticket. He lives with his wife and their pet dog in a two-bedroom house in London. He doesn't even owe anyone any money. Ordinary, through and through."

"So why was he used to raid the bank?" muttered Queen Bee.

"And who or what is Firestorm?" said Alfred Berners.

"I've cross-checked databases worldwide," said Simon. "There are no known criminals or terrorist groups using that name. Why Jones wrote it on the floor is another unknown at this stage."

"Keep digging," said Queen Bee.

The mechanical hands carefully unhooked the clasp that held the briefcase shut. The professor's face was a mask of concentration.

"Are the SWARM repaired?" said Queen Bee, watching the hands at work. Slowly, they opened the top of the case by a few centimetres.

"Almost," said Simon. He indicated a nearby tank. Inside, a thick, glowing purple liquid swirled around Chopper, Hercules, Sabre, Widow and Nero. The robots were held in a metal web. "We're dissolving the last of that glue. Luckily it didn't cause much mechanical damage – tougher exoskeleton coatings were one of the professor's latest upgrades. They'll withstand even bomb blasts now. He's also installed those faster data analysis programs Alfred designed, and he's given them a basic way to get around signal jammers, like the one they encountered during the Operation Sting incident. Only a fibre-optic

network, I'm afraid, but anything more would require too much power."

"What's the assessment of that glue, then?" said Queen Bee, still watching the mechanical hands. Delicately, they took hold of the sides of the briefcase, and turned it over.

"Our theory is that it's preprogrammed to solidify when it hits something, but we've no idea how that's possible. Those blobs even melted the tiny control circuits that the robots detected inside them, once they'd done their job. So they couldn't be traced, we assume. I've taken the bugs offline for the time being. Morph is recharging."

Professor Miller sent one of the mechanical hands into the briefcase. The hand moved very slowly and carefully.

Suddenly, the briefcase emitted a high-pitched tone. From inside came a flash of light and a sharp crackle of electricity. Everyone stood back a little in alarm, even though the force field was keeping them perfectly safe.

The briefcase burst into flames. White smoke filled the force field and within seconds, all that remained were the stolen bars of gold, sitting in the middle of a heap of ashes.

"Hmm, well," muttered the professor, slightly embarrassed, "at least we can give the bank its gold back."

"Everything was booby trapped to self-destruct if anyone messed with it," said Simon. "You've almost got to admire this Firestorm lot; they're very, very clever."

"Thank goodness Agent K was sensible enough not to open it at the scene!" said Alfred Berners.

Queen Bee looked thoughtful. "Well, whoever Firestorm are, they don't need to be clever to realize that their plan failed."

"Surely," said the professor, "they'd have had more chance of success if they'd used their technology to steal the gold quietly. At night, perhaps, or by tunnelling into the vault. They must have known that a dramatic assault like that would bring the police to the scene immediately."

"My guess is that they were totally confident of getting away with it," said Queen Bee. "It was only SWARM that stopped them. Just."

"They must have *wanted* to create panic and

get maximum attention," said Simon. "They're not simply high-tech bank robbers."

"No, there's more to it that that," agreed Queen Bee. "But at least we can deduce one thing: if they're stealing gold, they must be in need of more funds."

Simon nodded. "Gear like that doesn't come cheap."

"Anyway," said Queen Bee, "let's hope they've retreated to lick their wounds for the time being. I've got our human agents keeping an eye on police activity. The police are watching other banks closely, in case there's a second attack. This Firestorm won't catch them napping a second time."

3:10 p.m.

The immense stone structure of the MI6 building loomed up above the banks of the Thames. Traffic and pedestrians hurried along at ground level and nobody took any notice of a young woman, wearing glasses and a pink coat, who was heading south across Vauxhall Bridge. She was simply part of the crowd.

She walked quickly and steadily, but her eyes were glazed and unfocused.

Suddenly, a tiny light blinked on the arm of her glasses. The lenses darkened and began to scroll information. One switched to heat-sensitive vision, the other to infra-red.

The young woman reached into the pocket of her coat and pressed a switch. With a low hiss, jets built into the hem of the coat fired up. A second later, the jets roared to full power. The woman flew vertically into the air. Several people near her shrieked in fright.

A circular control pad lit up at the front of her coat. Using one hand, she guided her flight, aiming directly at the MI6 building. Behind her, cries of astonishment drifted up from the pavements.

Her speed through the air suddenly increased. She shot forward, her flight path taking her towards a large window on the building's ninth floor.

She reached out with her free hand. A large

nozzle whirred from her sleeve and in a burst of smoke, it fired a series of rockets. Her arm moved in a circular motion, guiding the rockets into a perfect ring.

They hit the building. A deafening explosion sent glass and stone bursting out across the Thames. The debris cascaded down the front of the building. Alarms and sirens sounded.

The woman shot towards the enormous gap that had been made in the ninth floor. She flew inside, the lenses of her glasses adjusting to allow her to see amidst the dust and smoke.

As the jets in her coat powered down with a whine, she raised her arm again and an ultrasonic pulse fired from a disc in the palm of her hand. The interior wall ahead of her shattered. Shouts and screams could be heard coming from nearby.

She stepped across the mounds of broken rubble, which now littered the floor. On the other side of the broken wall was a room packed with touchscreen PCs and wardrobe-sized computer servers.

An MI6 agent, coughing and covered in dust, managed to stagger into her line of sight. He pulled a revolver from the holster inside his jacket and aimed it at her. "Halt! Drop your weapons!"

A crackling blue arc of electricity flashed from the woman's palm. The MI6 agent was blown backwards from the force of it. He fell, knocked unconscious, his gun clattering and spinning across the floor.

The woman took a small cube, about the size of her palm, out of her coat pocket. She placed it beside one of the computer servers.

A thin metal probe snaked out of the cube and burrowed into the server, its end rotating like a drill bit. A second later, lights began to glow on the side of the cube, turning from red to orange to green, moving further up the cube as it sucked in data from the computer, filling itself with information.

After a few moments it bleeped and the woman returned the cube to her pocket. Taking out a marker pen, she wrote in large, neat letters across the screen of the nearest PC:

THE *FIRESTORM* IS *COMING*

She turned to leave. Behind her, urgent voices could be heard coming from an adjoining room.

Without so much as a backwards glance, she powered up the jets inside her coat. They quickly hissed into life, their droning sound rapidly getting louder and more high-pitched.

Half a dozen agents burst into the server room. The woman shot away through the gap she'd blown in the side of the building. The agents fired at her, again and again, but already she was gone. She flew north at high speed, across the river and away.

"We're tracking," said Simon Turing.

"Has anyone else got her? Police? MI5?" said Queen Bee.

"No, we're using the GPS systems Alfred reprogrammed himself. We're the only ones who can follow such a small target at low altitude."

In the SWARM laboratory, Simon was staring at a 3D display that floated above the workbench. A tiny dot was racing across a map of London, while detailed information ticked along below.

"Once again, Firestorm is confident of success," said Queen Bee. "They don't realize that an organization like SWARM even exists, let alone that we can follow their movements. They'll have assumed they could lose this woman somewhere in the city."

"Two attacks in less than two hours," said Alfred Berners, tapping at his laptop. "They're certainly confident."

"Any update on what was taken?" said Queen Bee.

"Working on it," said Simon. "Obviously, MI6 don't want to let on. Every last byte of it will be top secret. Many of their own staff don't even have access to those computers. Alfred's hacking into their network now. They've got a whole series of firewalls, but we should be able to find out what was taken before long."

"Can we launch the SWARM?" said Queen Bee.

Professor Miller checked the tank containing the robots. The purple liquid was draining away. "Three minutes," he said. "The repair systems will return them to launch positions automatically."

The synthesized voices of the robots all chimed from the speaker built into the workbench. "Rebooting. Full program and subroutine check underway."

"We may not have three minutes," muttered Queen Bee. "Where's the woman now?"

Simon's gaze was firmly on the 3D display. "She's weaving around just above roof level, keeping out of sight as far as possible... Still travelling at speed... Wait, she's slowing down... Altitude decreasing... She's entered the top floor of a multi-storey car park, bearing 314.5."

"Have we got anyone in that area?" said Queen Bee.

"Checking... Agent K isn't close, but I can divert Agent J. He's on his way to collect Sirena."

"Do it!"

3:21 p.m.

The young woman fired down her jetpack and landed in a dark corner on the empty upper level of a multi-storey car park. A cold breeze whipped round the stairwells and, beside her, water dripped through a crack in the low ceiling.

Suddenly, a large white hatchback sped into view. Its engine growled as it drove up a nearby ramp and approached the woman. The brakes of the car squealed as it came to a halt less than a metre in front of her. Leaving the engine running, a man in a tatty denim jacket and a black woollen beanie got out of the rusting vehicle. He had piercing pale blue eyes, and his mouth was set into a permanent line of disapproval.

He held out his hand. "Code Name Firestorm, Part Two," he said.

The woman reached into her pocket, took out the cube she'd used in the MI6 building and handed it over. Then she took off her gadget-filled coat and glasses, and handed them over too.

"Confirm timed memory wipe," he said.

"Confirmed," she said flatly.

He looked at his watch. "Less than a minute until it wears off," he muttered. "Perfect."

He got back into his car and sped away down the exit ramp. Almost as soon as the sound of

the vehicle faded away, the woman blinked and shook her head.

Within seconds, another car appeared, this one dark and sleek. The man who got out was dressed in a smart suit. It was Agent J. He tapped at his smartphone as he hurried over to the woman.

"Target acquired," he said. "Looks like she's either ditched the tech or it's been taken from her."

"What's going on?" cried the woman, rubbing her head. "Where am I?"

"It's OK," said Agent J. "Don't worry, you're safe. What's your name?"

"Sally," she said. "Sally Burns. What's the time? I'm going to be late for work, my shift at SuperSave starts at eleven. How did I get here? Who are you?"

"You're in safe hands now. I'm sorry, but I need to ask you: what's the last thing you remember?"

"What? Er, I was just leaving my flat. And then... It's a blank." Her voice rose in alarm. "What's going on here?"

Agent J quietly scanned her with his smartphone, which was filled with electronics specially adapted by Professor Miller and Alfred Berners.

He contacted HQ again. "It's gone. The data has gone."

"Acknowledged, Agent J," said Queen Bee, back at SWARM HQ. "Get whatever information you can from this woman, hand her over to the police, then return to base."

She stabbed at her phone in frustration, then turned to Professor Miller. "Time to step up our investigation," she said. "Launch the SWARM."

A series of intricate metal cages, about the size of a shoebox, rose up from the surface of the lab workbench. Inside each was a fully repaired micro-robot.

Red and green lights pulsed inside the cages. A glow flickered across nests of circuits and activation chimes sounded. The robots began to move.

"Online," they said as one.

CHAPTER THREE

3:40 p.m.

Two black sports cars came to a stop in two ordinary residential streets in London. One parked close to the home of Tim Jones, the teacher who'd carried out the bank raid. Several miles away, the other car was outside the block of flats where Sally Burns lived.

The first car was driven by SWARM's Agent J, the second by Agent K. Both of them reached across and entered a code into a touchscreen on their car's dashboard.

CODE NAME FIRESTORM

Beneath the cars, small hatches slid open. Inside were plastic blocks, moulded to fit individual SWARM robots. The robots detached themselves and dropped to the ground. Their mission: to search the homes of the two Firestorm "attackers" and unearth whatever they could. As soon as the robots were clear, the cars sped away, back to SWARM HQ.

Assigned to Tim Jones's house were Chopper, Hercules and Sirena. Widow, Nero, Sabre and Morph scuttled, flew and spun their way up to Sally Burns's flat.

"Flow sensor data through our communications network," signalled Chopper. "We can cross-check information as we go, and Simon Turing will monitor back at HQ."

"Logged," replied the others.

"Scans show no humans in the flat," transmitted Nero. "We are proceeding to the second floor. Entry through letter box."

"Nobody home here either," said Sirena. "Point of entry, dog flap at the rear of the house."

The robots's sensors were programmed to read, record and analyze everything around them.

Data streamed through their electronic brains: infra-red and X-ray scans, airborne particle sampling, chemical probes and high-res imaging.

Carbon-fibre legs tipped with micro-grips enabled them to skitter along any surface. Tiny sections of their metallic bodies housed specialized circuits and detectors. Chopper's compound eyes glittered as the mechanisms behind them whirred. Morph's gelatinous exoskeleton flattened as he squeezed into the tightest spaces.

Simon Turing's voice dropped into the network. "HQ to Hive 1 and Hive 2. We're getting a steady data feed. Keep looking."

"Why haven't the police searched here for clues already?" signalled Sabre.

"Queen Bee has control of the investigation," said Chopper. "The secret services are able to take over from the police at times like this, as Agent K did at the bank. My communications data says the human expression 'pulling rank' applies here."

"Besides," said Nero, "we can do the job with greater speed and efficiency than any human."

"Checking Tim Jones's laptop," said Sirena. "Hard drive is six terabytes. Scanning… Completed. Language analysis of documents shows nothing unusual."

"Scanning through mixed pile of papers and address books in Sally Burns's kitchen drawer," said Morph. "Some overdue bills, but nothing significant. Records of a charity walk… A camera containing twenty-three photos from a birthday party, dated four weeks ago…"

"Analyze," signalled Chopper. "Now that we've made a first set of basic scans, we can compare results and find out if anything connects Jones and Burns. There must be a reason why Firestorm used these two people to carry out attacks, rather than anyone else."

"Logged," replied the others.

"Tapping into government, police and local authority records," said Nero. His advanced programs hacked quickly and stealthily into a dozen official databases. "No links between them established. Different backgrounds, different jobs. It's highly unlikely that they've ever even passed each other on the street."

"Gathering inventories," said Sirena.

The micro-robots scurried and buzzed quietly around rooms, under doors and up stairs. Even if Tim Jones and Sally Burns had been at home, instead of in police custody, it was unlikely they would have noticed that the insects were there. They certainly wouldn't have realized that every object, piece of furniture and speck of dust in their homes was being counted and listed at lightning speed.

"Interesting," said Hercules. "Most people have certain things in common. Toothbrushes, socks, family photos, and so on. Once we eliminate all that, these two specific people have three factors that might link them. First: they both like the colour blue. Clothes, decoration, soft furnishings…"

"That's unlikely to be relevant," said Nero. "Humans can't see the full electromagnetic spectrum, like us. They only have a limited number of colours to choose from."

"A colour doesn't seem a likely link to crime, either," said Sirena.

"True," said Hercules. "Second: they've both

travelled to France, America and Spain within the last five years."

"Calculations of probability show that's a coincidence, but not a significant one," said Nero.

"Agreed," said Sirena. "Lots of people travel abroad. Checking online tourism data… France is the most visited country in the world, the United States is second, and Spain is fourth. It's a coincidence that both Jones and Burns like travelling, but those destinations are very likely ones. Many regular tourists will probably have been to all three."

"What's the third possible link?" said Nero.

"That's the most interesting of all," said Hercules. "I think this one shows a definite connection…"

3:51 p.m.

Back at SWARM's underground HQ, Queen Bee was at her desk. She was about to leave her office when the large screen in front of her announced

that a call was coming through. She tapped at the screen, and a scowling face appeared.

"I asked to be put through to whoever had taken over this operation," sneered the caller. "I might have known it would be you."

Queen Bee felt like dropping her head into her hands, but she stayed calm and confident.

It was Agent Morris Drake, MI5's Inland Containment Officer. He was a short, round man, with a scornful expression and a moustache that hid his upper lip. He didn't approve of any secret service activity that, like SWARM, was kept hidden even from MI5 and MI6.

"Still hiding behind your 'Top Secret' classification, are you?" he said. "Or are you prepared to tell me your name now? Or the name of your section?"

"You know I can't do that," replied Queen Bee. "Rest assured, this operation is—"

"Forgive me if I find your assurances rather hollow," said Drake icily. "My section should be handling this!"

"Why, exactly?" said Queen Bee calmly.

"Because, unlike you, I don't hide in the

shadows," sneered Drake. "Because, unlike you, I must be seen to operate within the law. Because, unlike you, I can reassure the public that I'm working on their behalf. Need I go on? I assume you're aware that this Firestorm thing is all over the media?"

"I am," said Queen Bee. "Now if you'll excuse me, I was about to brief my team and—"

"Oh, 'brief your team', eh? Well, that'll get the job done, I'm sure."

"Unlike some, we find teamwork very effective," smiled Queen Bee.

Agent Drake leaned forward. "This is a mainland UK matter, and that means MI5 should handle it. Is that clear?"

"While Firestorm remains a mystery," said Queen Bee, "my agents are in a better position to investigate. Whatever Firestorm may be, it uses technology that's way beyond the experience of the police, or MI6. Or even, believe it or not, you."

"But not these mysterious agents of yours," said Drake. "Or so you claim. How do we know that anything you say can be trusted?"

"All I know, Agent Drake," said Queen Bee

patiently, "is that every moment we sit here arguing is a moment lost in our hunt for Firestorm."

"I'm going to be putting my own people on this," said Drake, "no matter what you say. You know I will. I've done it before."

"You don't even have access to the data that was stolen from MI6," said Queen Bee. "You have no idea what you're looking for."

"And neither do you!" snapped Drake. "MI6 keep that stuff wrapped up tighter than a mouse in the coils of a boa constrictor. Nobody knows what was nicked – don't try to bluff me!"

The screen went black. Queen Bee shut her eyes for a second to control her temper, then headed for the laboratory. When she arrived, Simon Turing was at the 3D display, monitoring the progress of the robots.

"Why would Drake want to get involved in this?" Alfred asked, when Queen Bee finished telling them about the phone call. "His section can't have any clue what's going on. That's why the home secretary has put SWARM in charge, isn't it?"

"Surely Drake's just setting himself up to look

foolish. Again," added Professor Miller.

"I agree," said Queen Bee. "However, we must take his threats seriously. The only reason we've been given the go-ahead to control this case is our success on past missions. We can't afford any slip-ups. The government is very twitchy about Firestorm and might easily hand the case over to someone else if we don't make rapid progress. The prime minister and the home secretary are concerned about the media coverage."

"It's all over the web and the TV news channels," said Alfred. "One minute they're playing up the bank-robbery angle, the next they're claiming that Firestorm is some sort of terrorist organization, because of the attack on MI6. All the coverage is making the public very nervous indeed."

"Which is exactly what Firestorm wants," said Queen Bee. "Everything's been done to create as much havoc as possible. If only we knew why!"

"I'm puzzled by their choice of targets so far," said Professor Miller. "Why steal gold, and then steal data? What are they after, precisely?"

"Ah!" said Alfred with a smile. "Nero worked that one out while the robots were being transported to their current locations. He said he'd been observing humans long enough to calculate the most likely probabilities. Firestorm's main objective must be connected to the theft of the data. You don't break into a secret-service building filled with highly trained spies just for fun, even if you do want to make a splash. There are many ways to get attention that don't involve making MI6 your target. So the data must be Firestorm's number one priority. The gold is secondary. They could have raided any bank, if they needed funds. Firestorm attacked that particular one simply because it would draw maximum publicity."

"We've already established that those weapons will have cost a small fortune," said Queen Bee. "What's the assessment on that?"

"Nero's calculations suggest that an attempted bank robbery marks Firestorm out as a small organization," said Alfred. "A large group, or a hostile foreign government, would have more resources."

"Could it be an individual acting alone?" said Queen Bee.

Alfred wrinkled his nose. "I suppose it's

possible. Whoever they are, Firestorm must be extremely serious about their objectives."

"Which brings us back to the data," said the Professor. "Did you manage to hack into MI6?"

"Oh yes, no problem," said Alfred brightly. "It took a little longer than expected, but my reprogrammed computer virus has been burrowing through their network for an hour now. In fact, the results should be accessible in a moment or two."

He tapped at a screen beside him. Information began to flow across it.

"At least we now know what the stolen data is," said Queen Bee. She remembered the end of her conversation with Drake and smiled to herself.

Alfred looked thoughtful. "It's not good news. Firestorm knew exactly what they were doing. The data they took could only be retrieved in that one room. It was totally separate from the mainframe. That cube of theirs targeted the exact servers it needed."

"It seems Firestorm are remarkably well informed," said Queen Bee. "You know, I think we may have to consider the possibility that they

have a mole inside the secret service. What was the extent of the theft?"

Alfred looked up from the screen. He chose his words carefully. "They took the names and addresses of every MI6 agent currently operating abroad. Plus, the names of everyone MI6 suspects of being an agent for a foreign government. Tagged to the names were details of every mission they've been sent on, every fake ID they've used, and every contact they have in the world's security services."

"Good grief," muttered Professor Miller.

"If they put information like that online," said Queen Bee. "It would destroy our entire spy network, worldwide. Every agent's life would be in danger. Every government around the world, friend or enemy, would know the details of MI6's activities."

"I'm afraid that's not all," said Alfred. "They took details of some of MI5's activities too. MI6 missions sometimes overlap MI5's. Firestorm are in possession of a full MI5 staff list."

"Do they know about us as well?" said Professor Miller.

"No," said Alfred. "Because we're part of the SIA, our secrecy level is above almost everything else. However, we're now the only branch of the secret service Firestorm's got nothing on."

"Then that remains our main advantage," said Queen Bee. "They'll have no idea that it's us they're up against. Our mission objectives are clear: we must track down Firestorm before they can use that stolen data. If the data gets out into the open, I dread to think what will happen."

"Even a small leak of secrets can cause a major international row," said Alfred.

"Quite," said Queen Bee. "If this data is released, we could see wars break out all over the world. At the very least, our own government could end up at war with any number of enemies. Every country knows there are spies, but no country wants to admit that foreign agents are spying on *them*. This is a race against time. Right now, we need our robots like never before."

At that moment, Simon Turing looked up from the 3D display. "Ms Maynard," he said to Queen Bee. "I think the SWARM has discovered something very interesting…"

CHAPTER FOUR

4:00 p.m.

"Cashier number four, please."

The recorded voice was loud and cheery. The long, snaking queue shuffled forward a little. Everything was as normal in this small north London branch of the Lowfax Building Society.

Cashier number four smiled at her next customer from behind a bulletproof screen. "Hello, my name's Sue. How can I help you today?"

The customer was an old lady, quite short and

thin, wearing a thick coat, gloves and a woolly hat. Her eyes seemed slightly unfocused.

"Can I help you, madam?" said Sue. "Are you all right?"

The old lady paused for a moment, as if she was listening to something nobody else could hear. She leaned close to the screen. "Give me all your money," she said quietly.

"I beg your pardon?" The cashier blinked.

"Give me all your money," repeated the old lady. She slid a fold-out shopping bag into the metal tray beneath the cashier's screen. "Fill this. Notes only, no coins. Do it quickly. Do it quietly. If you try to press your alarm button, I'll know."

Sue half-laughed. "Sorry, is this a wind-up? Are we on telly?"

A small hatch opened at the front of the old lady's hat. The barrel of a gun suddenly whirred out and the tiny spot of a laser sight appeared over the cashier's heart.

"Fill the bag," said the old lady. "Now."

The cashier gulped. She had no idea whether the woman was bluffing or not. Then she remembered the reports about weird robberies in the City that were all over the news.

She took the bag and slowly opened it out. The customers behind the old lady in the queue hadn't noticed anything strange yet. Neither had the other cashiers.

The dot of the laser sight followed the cashier as she moved. She opened up the bag, then opened a set of three drawers beside her. Each drawer contained large amounts of cash, neatly sorted into plastic compartments. Sue began to place the cash into the bag.

"Faster," said the old lady quietly. "Get more from the safe behind you."

Trying to stay calm, Sue swung round on her chair. There was a hefty safe, about the size of a wardrobe, standing against the wall a few metres away. She pressed a six-digit combination into the safe's key coder and it opened. Inside were shelves packed with papers, files and plastic wrappers filled with money. Nervously, Sue began to take out the wrappers and place them in the shopping bag.

She glanced across to the other cashiers. One of them had heard the safe opening, and was looking at Sue with a puzzled expression on her face. Sue shot a wide-eyed look back at her, to indicate that there was something wrong.

The other cashier took the hint. Calmly, she reached out under her desk with her foot. The toe of her shoe tapped along, feeling for the alarm button that was located close to the floor.

Suddenly, motion-detection systems inside the old lady's coat began to beep. Instantly, she pulled from her pocket what looked like a black tennis ball. She flung it at the floor in front of her.

As the ball hit the floor, an electro-magnetic pulse rippled out. The alarm buttons underneath the cashiers' desks all fused and sparked. So did every electronic device within fifty metres, except the specially shielded ones carried by the old lady. The customers who were using their smartphones all yelped and dropped them in surprise.

The old lady reached out and touched the cashier's bulletproof screen. Tiny lights blinked on the fingers of her gloves. Suddenly the screen burst into a shower of tiny pieces.

"Give!" demanded the old lady.

The laser sight was still levelled at Sue's heart. Terrified, she pushed the nearly full shopping bag over the destroyed screen.

The old lady grabbed it and hurried out into the street. The customers behind her in the queue were too shocked to do anything. The cashiers were trapped, because the electric locks on all the doors had fused. After a minute or two, Sue crawled over her broken screen.

"Call the police, someone!" she cried, rushing into the street. She looked left and right, but there was no sign of the thief.

The old lady was gone. She'd ducked into a narrow alley close to the building society, and used a gripping device from her coat to raise a heavy manhole cover. Within seconds, she had climbed down into the drainage system below, and the manhole cover had been pulled back into place above her. Written on the pavement outside the building society, were the words:

THE FIRESTORM IS ABOUT TO IGNITE

"SWARM HQ to Hive 1, report," said Queen Bee.

"Hive 1 to HQ," signalled Chopper. "We think we've found something that links Tim Jones and Sally Burns. We've cross-checked every item in their homes, and have discovered that they both own exactly the same make and model of wireless speakers."

"Speakers for a sound system?" said Queen Bee.

"Affirmative,"

"Is that really significant?" said Queen Bee. "Pick any two adults at random, and you may find a match on the brand of phone they own, or where they buy most of their clothes, all sorts of things."

"Hive 2 to HQ," cut in Nero. "That's true, Queen Bee, but these particular speakers are a model not generally sold in this country, and which are normally expensive to buy."

"Surely all this tells us is that they're both music fans? They've bought top-quality equipment because they value what they listen to?"

"That might be the case," said Nero, "if it were not for something else shown by our inventory of their possessions. Neither of them owns a large amount of music, or any other audio material."

"A human who'd consider themselves a music fan would own a lot," said Chopper. "Scans of hard drives, iPods and physical CDs shows that Jones owns only two thousand, one hundred and eleven music tracks, while Burns owns only two thousand, four hundred and eighty-five."

"That sounds quite a lot," said Queen Bee.

"These are less than average amounts for adult humans of their ages and income levels," said Nero. "I have checked with a number of online databases."

"The presence of these specific speakers in the homes of humans who don't collect audio tracks is a statistical oddity," said Chopper.

"It's not much to go on," said Queen Bee, "but you should investigate further. Wait! We're picking up reports here of a third raid by Firestorm. Keep sending data back to the lab, I'll be in touch shortly."

"Logged, Queen Bee," replied the robots.

The SWARM team at Tim Jones's house – Chopper the dragonfly, Hercules the stag beetle and Sirena the butterfly – made their way over to the shelf in the sitting room where the two speakers sat.

Over at Sally Burns's flat, the second team – Nero the scorpion, Sabre the mosquito, Morph the centipede and Widow the spider – had located the speakers on the floor of the flat's main living area, at either end of a sofa that was littered with cushions and magazines.

The speakers themselves didn't look unusual or remarkable. They were plain, black and box-like. There was a manufacturer's badge showing the make and model number "BebKo-X1" in the lower-left corner of each.

"Comparing X-ray scans shows that all these speakers contain exactly the same components and circuits," said Sirena at Tim Jones's house.

"Confirmed," said Nero at Sally Burns's flat. "They connect to a Wi-Fi system using a standard set of protocols."

"Same over here," said Hercules. "Status check: no human activity detected nearby."

"Police databases show both Jones and Burns are still being held in custody," added Nero.

"Beginning high-res scans of individual circuits inside the speakers..." said Sirena. "There's something strange here. Nero, do you read a data-static feedback loop too?"

"Affirmative," said Nero. "In fact, there's an entire circuit board that's not part of the speaker system itself."

"Confirmed," said Sirena.

"We were right," said Morph. "These speakers are definitely a clue of some kind."

"Should we neutralize them?" said Sabre.

"Not until we know what we've found here," said Chopper. "Let's take a close look at these circuit boards."

The robots calculated and analyzed, as sensor data flowed through their electronic brains.

"Each speaker has had one small extra circuit board added to it," said Sirena. "Connectors and soldering marks show that this addition was made recently."

"Someone has taken these speakers, opened them up, and modified them," said Chopper.

"Whoever is behind the attacks, most likely."

"I'd say these extra circuits were home-made," said Nero. "Extraordinary. Firestorm may be one individual acting alone after all."

"That would indeed be extraordinary," said Sirena.

"I meant it's extraordinary that I could have been wrong about Firestorm," said Nero. "I calculate that the circuits were home-made because these components are the same, but there are very small differences in exactly where and how they've been fitted into the speakers. For example, the extra circuit in this speaker at Burns's flat has been mounted eight millimetres lower than the one you're looking at there in Jones's house. That probably wouldn't happen if the circuits had been added in a factory. Everything there would be done in a standard way. Someone has assembled these circuits individually, and wired them inside the speakers too. This is something human agents might have taken weeks to spot."

"If I didn't know better," said Hercules, "I'd say you were boasting."

"This evidence is important," said Chopper. "It's too much of a coincidence that we've found these speakers, modified in this way, in the homes of both Jones and Burns."

"The question is why?" said Hercules. "What do these extra circuits actually do? Why have they been wired into ordinary audio speakers? A data-static feedback loop would seem to serve no function at all here."

"The added circuits aren't even powered up," said Sirena. "The speakers are on standby, but these strange extras appear completely inactive."

"I'll cut my way inside this speaker," said Hercules. "We need to get one of these circuits free and take it back to the lab at SWARM HQ."

"Logged," replied the others.

"Be careful," said Morph.

Hercules's razor-sharp claw was designed to cut through almost anything. It clicked and whirred as the targeting systems in his brain homed in on a small area at the back of the speaker.

"I'll make a hole where it's least likely to be noticed," he said.

His claw sliced quickly into the speaker's

tough plastic case. Within a few seconds, he'd cut a neat, circular hole, exactly large enough for his wing case to fit through. He crawled inside the speaker, pulling his legs in tightly. He was the bulkiest of the SWARM robots, even though he was only five centimetres long.

"I see it," he reported from inside. "It's a very advanced piece of work. Whoever made it was also extremely careful – there are no fingerprints on any of the components. I'll remove it now."

He scuttled alongside the circuit board. His sharp claw moved to snip the board free.

Suddenly, there was a sharp crackling sound. A flash of white light shone through the hole Hercules had made. Inside the speaker, sparks flew from the robot's joints. Wisps of smoke rose around his claw, and his legs curled sharply inward.

"He's offline!" said Chopper.

"The circuit was booby-trapped!" said Morph. "Exactly like the briefcase Tim Jones had in the bank. It must have a hidden power source."

The robots couldn't detect any electrical activity in Hercules. All his systems were dead.

Folding back their wings, Chopper and Sirena wriggled through the hole in the speaker. Hercules was silent, surrounded by smoke and the smell of burning.

At that moment, a clunking sound came from the back of Tim Jones's house. There was a scuffling and a series of bumps.

"Someone's entering the house," said Chopper.

"Scanning…" said Sirena. "It's Tim Jones's wife and their pet dog."

"Get out of there," said Morph. "Now!"

"Police confirm a third raid," announced Simon Turing. "This time, Firestorm got away with almost half a million pounds!"

Every screen in SWARM's laboratory was filled with scrolling information. Queen Bee narrowed her eyes as she watched the displays.

"Do we have any leads?"

"Sorry, Ms Maynard," said Simon. "CCTV went down inside and outside the building. Some sort of signal blocker, I assume. We have no visual on the attacker, apart from a verbal description. She vanished into thin air."

Queen Bee turned to Alfred Berners. "Update?"

"My hacks into MI6 are holding. It seems that secret-service departments all over the world are starting to panic, not knowing who Firestorm are, or what their objective is. MI6 have put every agent outside the UK on full alert. Security forces worldwide are bracing for similar attacks: the CIA in America, the MSS in China, Russia's FSB, everyone. They're all very jumpy. Accusations and suspicions are beginning to fray nerves and shorten tempers. On top of all that, the media are going crazy now there's been a third attack."

Queen Bee took a deep breath. "We must handle this with extreme caution. The world could collapse into war even quicker than we feared. Simon, what can the robots give us?"

"Hercules's signal just went down."

"What?"

Simon tapped at a nearby screen. A beep confirmed that the SWARM network was live.

"SWARM HQ to Hive 1," said Queen Bee.

"What's happened?"

"Nothing we can't handle, Queen Bee," said Chopper. "Hercules has been damaged by a power surge. He's fused to a circuit board and it will take time to free him."

"Do you need Agent K or Agent J to intervene?"

"Negative, Queen Bee. The Firestorm situation is too urgent, they're needed for the investigation. The logical thing to do is leave Hercules here until we can return for him. He is safely hidden inside this speaker, there's no danger of discovery."

"I agree," said Queen Bee. "We need every agent we've got on this, human or robot."

"A human has returned to the house now. Sirena and I will keep out of sight, exit the house and fly directly back to HQ."

"Understood." Queen Bee turned her attention to the second group. "HQ to Hive 2."

"We're leaving Burns's flat now," signalled Nero. "No problem here. We'll proceed to the pick-up point."

"Acknowledged. HQ out," said Queen Bee.

She turned to Simon Turing. "Any good news?"

"Actually, yes," said Simon. "The robots have

gathered a massive amount of data from the homes of Jones and Burns. I've just run it through our own computers. Look at what's coming up on the 3D display. I think we may have exactly the breakthrough we need!"

On the display were detailed diagrams of the mysterious speakers. Beside the diagrams, streams of information were being divided into categories by SWARM's computers.

"The robots identified those speakers as imported," said Simon, "so we've compiled a full list of every shop and warehouse in the UK that bought that make and model. There aren't many. Better still, the scans taken by the robots have given us an exact breakdown of the components used to make those weird added circuits: microchips, PCBs, memristors, capacitors, all that sort of stuff. We can identify everyone who's bought those specific components too. A full cross-check of all this information gives us eleven places that have bought both the speakers and the added components. All of them are small electrical shops. One of them is sure to lead us to Firestorm."

"Good work!" said Queen Bee. "We'll start checking them immediately."

"No need," smiled Simon. "So far, all the attacks have taken place in London. There's only one shop on the list within fifty miles of all three raids. That's most likely to be our Firestorm link."

"Excellent, where is it?"

"In a side street off Tottenham Court Road, a small audio sales and repair place called Trendi Soundz."

4:38 p.m.

A buzzer sounded over the Trendi Soundz shop door as the old lady entered. Her eyes were still slightly glazed.

The shop was small and cluttered. Shelves and racks were stacked full of boxes of audio equipment, cables, speakers and modems. There were flash-shaped signs cut out of bright orange card with handwritten text in black marker pen advertising "Lowest Pricez" and "Best Bargainz".

There were no customers inside and the shop's owner sat behind a dusty wooden counter. He was a middle-aged man in a tatty denim jacket and a black woollen beanie. A radio was in pieces on the counter, and he was working on it with a screwdriver. He looked up as the buzzer sounded. He had piercing pale blue eyes.

"Ah," he said quietly. "Success."

The old lady said nothing. She placed the shopping bag on the counter. He glanced inside to check that it was filled with money, then tucked it away out of sight. The old lady placed her coat, hat and gloves on the counter too.

"Code name Firestorm, Part Three," said the shop owner. "Go across the street. Take the next bus, go three stops. Sit outside the nearest coffee shop. Memory wipe will take place one minute after you sit down."

"Confirmed," she said flatly.

"Good," he grinned. "Now go. You smell of drains."

CHAPTER FIVE

4:59 p.m.

SWARM's Agent K drew up her car outside a coffee shop close to Euston station. She had received an update by phone from HQ, then collected Widow, Nero, Sabre and Morph from the pick-up point near Sally Burns's flat. The robots were back in the travel pod underneath the car. Now Agent K had been diverted here, to pick up Firestorm's third innocent victim.

"You're sure that's her?" said Agent K.

Nero's voice was relayed through the car radio. "I tapped into the city's traffic-control CCTV network. I checked every camera inside Greater London. Her age fits the verbal description given to the police. Visual analysis of her facial expression and body language show she is in a confused state of mind, and sensors currently indicate she has a raised heartbeat. All factors, taken together, logically suggest she is the one."

A moment later, Agent K sat down at one of the coffee shop's outside tables, beside the old lady who'd just delivered the bag of money to Trendi Soundz.

"I'm sorry to bother you," she said. "Are you by any chance wondering how you got here?"

"I am," said the old lady. "I don't even like coffee. Who are you?"

"I'm working alongside the police." Agent K showed her ID, which identified her as a member of the secret services. "Have you heard of Firestorm?"

"Those robberies earlier on?" Her eyes widened. "You're not saying they got me to do one, like the other two people, are ya?"

"I'm afraid I am,"

"Those rotten… Oh dear, am I under arrest?"

"No," smiled Agent K. "The police will want to talk to you, but we know you were acting under some kind of hypnosis. You're not in trouble. What's your name?"

"Eileen. Eileen Parkins." She sniffed. "Can you smell drains?"

"I'll call and arrange for the local police to collect you in a few minutes. You can give them a statement. The earlier suspects have just been allowed to go home, so you shouldn't be kept long. One last question, Eileen. Do you know a shop called Trendi Soundz?"

"I do," said Eileen. "I got a sound system there – it was a really good deal. Why?"

"Just a routine enquiry."

5:15 p.m.

Agent J's car was parked in a long, narrow street off Tottenham Court Road, at a position that allowed a good view of Trendi Soundz. Chopper and Sirena were on the headrest of the passenger seat.

Agent J tapped his smartphone. "Agent K, what's your status?"

"Less than a minute from your position."

"Acknowledged," said Agent J. He opened a channel to HQ. "Hive 1 to SWARM HQ, we're in position."

"Anything happening there?" Queen Bee's voice sounded tense.

"Negative, Ms Maynard," said Agent J. "Nobody's come in or out of the shop. Sirena's keeping her sensors focused on the back of the building. No movement there either. Only one person inside. Do we have an ID yet?"

"Simon Turing's working on it now," said Queen Bee. "Trendi Soundz has been registered as a private company. The shop itself is a perfectly ordinary, legitimate business. However, the name of whoever owns it has been deliberately covered up. Several databases that ought to list the owner have had all record of Trendi Soundz deleted. Others have been changed, to list fake companies or fake identities."

"Curiouser and curiouser," muttered Agent J.

"That's a quotation," said Chopper. "Lewis Carroll, *Alice's Adventures in Wonderland,* 1865, Chapter Two."

"This adds to our suspicion that Firestorm has been getting help from inside the secret service, doesn't it?" said Agent J.

"Absolutely," said Queen Bee. "Only someone with access to a large number of official records could have hidden information about Trendi Soundz in this way. Politicians or senior police officers could have done it, but not without signing various pieces of paper. Only someone in the secret service could have done it on the quiet."

"So, do we have no idea who the shop owner is?" said Agent J.

"For the moment, no, but Simon and Alfred are confident they can track back through the affected databases and ID them soon."

"Is that why you want us to tread carefully, and not simply raid Trendi Soundz?"

"That's one reason, yes," said Queen Bee. "The other is our knowledge of Firestorm's tactics so far. They're using technology that's almost beyond what even we've got. They cover their tracks and they pack booby traps into everything. We have to handle things with the utmost care. That's why I want the robots leading the way. They can watch and act with more stealth than anyone else. Now we know about Trendi Soundz, we can nip any further attacks in the bud."

"Have you managed to keep Agent Drake and MI5 at arm's length?"

"So far, yes," said Queen Bee. "The prime minister and the home secretary are still giving SWARM full control of this crisis. But MI5 will be allowed to take over the investigation if we slip up. Agent Drake is grinding his teeth, waiting for a chance to take charge."

"Alert," cut in Sirena. "Adult male approaching the shop. It's Tim Jones."

"The teacher Firestorm hypnotized for the bank raid?" said Agent J. "The police only let him and Sally Burns go a little while ago. What's he doing here?"

"He may be involved with Firestorm after all," said Queen Bee.

"Chopper, listen in!" said Agent J.

"Logged," said Chopper.

The micro-robot dragonfly's wings buzzed into operation. He darted into the air, and out through the gap at the top of the passenger window.

At that moment, Agent K's car appeared at the end of the street. Without slowing down, or even acknowledging the presence of Agent J, she clicked the switch on her dashboard. The hatch on the travel pod fixed beneath her car opened, and Widow, Nero, Sabre and Morph dropped neatly onto the street. The car headed back towards SWARM HQ. Nero and Morph scuttled along the gutters. Widow fired an ultra-thin line at the closest building and swung up into the air. Sabre zipped over to Agent J.

"Looks like we got here at exactly the right time," he said, his voice routed through Agent J's smartphone.

Tim Jones was carrying a plastic supermarket carrier bag. There was a chunky rectangular shape inside it.

"One of the speakers," said Sirena. "Scanning... It's the one Hercules is in!"

"Stand by, everyone," said Agent J quietly.

Chopper landed on the shop's cluttered front window. Tim Jones went in. The buzzer above the door sounded automatically as he entered.

A tiny video probe jutted out from the underside of Chopper's head. It stuck itself onto the glass. Everything that went on in the shop could now be seen and heard on the SWARM network. Agent J watched on his phone.

Tim Jones approached the man at the counter. Eileen Parkins's coat, hat and gloves had been stored away, as had the shopping bag full of money.

"Yeah?" said the shop owner. At first, he barely looked up. As soon as he did, he made an almost comical double-take. He recognized Jones instantly. His piercing eyes darted past Jones's shoulder, checking that the man was alone.

"Hi," said Tim Jones. The tone of his voice registered on the robots' sensors as annoyed and irritable. "We bought a pair of these speakers from you a couple of weeks ago. This one's stopped working."

The shop owner didn't reply for a moment.

"He's wondering if this is a set-up," muttered Agent J. "He's wondering if Jones has remembered something, or worked out what happened to him."

"Why would this man have let those speakers remain in the homes of Jones, Burns and Parkins?" said Sabre. "The modified circuits in them are evidence. After all, they led *us* here. Why wouldn't he have set them to self-destruct, or something like that?"

"Why *not* leave them?" said Nero. "He couldn't possibly have predicted that micro-robot insects would investigate them. He could safely have assumed that his modified circuits would never be discovered. Remember, we don't yet know exactly what those circuits do."

"Hello?" said Tim Jones.

"Huh?" said the shop owner. "Oh, yeah. Sorry, mate. What was it?"

"I said, this speaker's stopped working."

The shop owner was clearly nervous. As he stood behind the counter, Chopper's eyes took a detailed close-up photo of him, and relayed it back to SWARM HQ to help Simon Turing ID the man.

"That's a BebKo-X1," he said.

"Yes, I know," grumbled Tim Jones. "You said they were top quality. I wondered why you were selling them at such a knock-down price. Was it a faulty batch, or something?"

The shop owner eyed Jones carefully. "He's still not sure what's going on," muttered Agent J, "but he's realized that Jones really does have a faulty speaker."

"When that circuit blew up and damaged Hercules," said Morph, "it must have damaged some of the speaker's other components too."

"Mr … Jones, right?" asked the shop owner.

"Yes," blinked Tim Jones. "That's well remembered."

"I like to look after my customers," said the man.

"Yes, well, I've been having a terrible day, and I got home—"

"Terrible? Why terrible?" said the shop owner casually.

"Umm, it doesn't matter, but I got home not long ago and I tried to put some music on, to calm my nerves, and this nearly new speaker

had simply stopped working. I've had it up to here today, I really have." He plonked the carrier bag containing the speaker onto the counter. "I wouldn't have bothered bringing it straight round like this, but it was the last straw."

The shop owner slowly opened the carrier bag and lifted out the speaker. He looked it over, but didn't appear to spot the small access hole made by Hercules.

"You haven't done anything to it, have you?" he said.

"Like what?" said Tim Jones.

"Dropped it?" shrugged the shop owner. "Put it close to a strong magnetic field? Taken the back off and poked around inside?"

"No, no, no, it's been sitting on the same shelf, undisturbed, since we got it," said Tim Jones.

"And your other one works?"

"Yes, it's fine."

Suddenly, Simon Turing's voice cut into the SWARM communications network. "HQ to Hive 1, we've got a match on the photo Chopper just sent us. The man's name is Henry Blackwater. We're delving into records now, but it looks like he's on

MI5's current watch list, so he must be a known criminal of some kind. We're sending Agent K to his home address."

"Logged," replied Chopper.

"Thanks HQ, Hive 1 out," said Agent J.

Henry Blackwater sniffed and placed the speaker behind the counter. "Yes, well, I've still got some of these in stock, I'll give you a free replacement."

"Oh," said Tim Jones, raising his eyebrows slightly at Blackwater's sudden change of heart. "OK. Thank you."

Blackwater sorted through a pile of boxes on a rack behind him. He pulled one out and handed it over. "There."

"Thanks," said Tim Jones. "Bye." He put the box into his carrier bag as he left the shop.

Blackwater watched him go. He moved to the far edge of the counter and craned his neck, to check that Jones was walking away and not reporting back to someone outside. He stood there for a few moments, eyeing the street outside. Agent J's car was well out of his line of sight.

He returned to the broken speaker. He put it

back on the counter, and turned it round a couple of times.

"Well now," he mumbled to himself. "What happened here? Lucky you didn't go wrong yesterday, eh?"

He fetched a set of miniature screwdrivers and spread them across the counter. He flipped the speaker over, turning its rear side upwards.

"Alert!" signalled Chopper. "It looks like he's going to open up the speaker. Hercules will be discovered."

"Already on it," said Agent J. He was out of his car and across the street in seconds. He dashed over to the shop, the rest of the SWARM robots scuttling and buzzing by his side. "Sirena, maintain a full sensor watch outside."

"Logged," said the butterfly. She fluttered down and landed on the wall above the shop's window.

Agent J marched into the shop, whistling loudly. The buzzer sounded. The noise and movement were enough of a distraction to allow the remaining five robots to enter the shop unnoticed.

"Hi!" said Agent J, raising a hand in greeting.

"We're just closing," said Blackwater impatiently.

"It'll only take a minute," Agent J replied cheerfully. "Promise. Need some expert advice!" His secret-service training has given him plenty of practice at adopting undercover identities.

"We're open tomorrow at nine," grumbled Blackwater.

"I don't mind paying full price," said Agent J. "Budget, no problem. Just point me in the direction of the top stuff and I'm out of your hair."

Blackwater sighed. "What is it you want?" He quietly slid the speaker and screwdrivers to one side.

"You're a star!" Agent J grinned. "I'm looking for one of those, er, what-they-called, where you can stream stuff from your phone and hear it all over the house?"

Blackwater nodded. "A network media player."

"Yeah, that's the one. I need the lot: speakers, player, you know. Will I need a new Wi-Fi router?"

"Not necessarily," said Blackwater. "What sort do you have now?"

While Agent J distracted Blackwater, the robots quietly headed for the speaker. Chopper and Sabre hovered along close to the ceiling, while Nero, Widow and Morph crawled up a rack and onto the counter.

"I've scanned a couple of items on these racks," said Nero. "One of them contains exactly the same sort of modified circuit board that we found in those speakers. It's inside a radio."

"I've found one too," said Morph. "There's a dock here with an identical circuit."

The robots' sensors quickly established that there were thirty-seven items in the shop which had also been altered. Almost all of them were expensive items on sale at unusually low prices.

"Blackwater must sell them to unsuspecting customers, who then become puppets for Firestorm," said Chopper.

Nero scurried up onto the broken speaker and through the hole Hercules had made. "I'll need some help getting Hercules free," he said. "He's bulkier than the rest of us!"

"It may be better if we all help," said Chopper. "We've got to get Hercules out of there as fast as possible. If Blackwater takes the back off the speaker and discovers that a micro-robot stag beetle is in there, our cover is blown. That must never happen."

Agent J was doing an excellent job of keeping Blackwater busy. He was getting Blackwater to open up boxes and show him various types of equipment.

Sirena, outside the shop, kept her sensors trained on the street, but there was nothing suspicious to report. She also monitored everything Blackwater was doing.

"You may not have long to free Hercules," she said. "Blackwater is getting noticeably impatient. He's probably itching to return to the speaker and find out why it broke down."

"Logged," said Chopper. All five robots were now inside the speaker. "Widow, seal the hole for the time being, just in case it's spotted."

"Logged," said Widow. She adjusted the settings of her thread-making mechanism and fired a coiling line of web at the hole that exactly matched the colour of the speaker casing. The thread formed a neat, flat plug.

Meanwhile, the robots made detailed scans of Hercules. "Four of his legs are fused into the circuit board," said Nero. "I can cut around the board, but it will take 42.9 seconds."

"It would be quicker to simply snip through the legs," said Sabre. "He can be repaired back at HQ."

"My pincers don't have enough power to do that," said Nero. "He's the toughest of us all. Hercules is built to withstand direct sledge-hammer blows and other explosive impacts."

"Also, we couldn't risk leaving even minor mechanical parts behind," said Chopper. "Anything like that might threaten the secrecy of SWARM."

"Whatever you do, do it quickly!" said Morph.

"Morph's right," said Sirena, from outside the shop. "Analysis of Blackwater's body language shows he's trying to get Agent J out of his shop."

Agent J was getting the same impression. Although, at that moment, he wasn't tapped into the robots' communications, he knew they'd need time to get Hercules out, but he could see that Blackwater was getting jittery.

"Have you decided? Only, like I said, I'm closing."

"Sorry, yeah," grinned Agent J. "What was the output of this system again? The silver one?"

"Look, I want to get home today, OK? If I leave too late, I hit the traffic."

"Sorry, sorry, yeah, you're right! I know I go on! My girlfriend's always telling me to shut up."

"I know how she feels," said Blackwater with a fake smile.

Inside the speaker, Nero's pincers were snipping into one end of the circuit board. At the other end, Morph was flattening himself to squeeze between the board and the speaker's casing, in order to force the two apart.

"We can't have more than a matter of seconds," said Chopper calmly.

"I think," said Agent J, "I'm going to go for … the silver one. No! The red one! No! The silver one, definitely."

Blackwater had lost patience. "Oh, make up your mind. Do you want to buy this thing or not?"

"Oh, I do, I do. You've been really helpful, Mr Blackwater. I'm so grateful for your expertise."

The robots spotted Agent J's error in less than a micro-second. Blackwater himself noticed it almost immediately. Agent J was so intent on keeping Blackwater busy that he didn't realize what he'd done.

"Can't we communicate with him?" said Nero.

"No, he was using his smartphone in the car," said Chopper. "There wasn't time for him to place an earpiece before we had to rush over here to the shop."

"He's in danger!" said Nero.

Blackwater reached over the counter and produced a set of chunky headphones. He put them on his head, shuffling them slightly to ensure a snug fit over his ears. "You're going for the silver one, then?" he said with a smile.

"Oh, yes, definitely," said Agent J. The headphones puzzled him, but before he could ask about them, Blackwater picked up the radio he'd been working on earlier. This was one of the items containing one of the mysterious extra circuits.

"We do some great radios," said Blackwater. "This is the latest digital receiver."

By now, Agent J was nervous. He'd spotted the change in Blackwater's attitude. A moment later, he realized the mistake he'd made. Blackwater had never mentioned his name.

"Thanks, I'll take the silver one, then," bluffed Agent J. "And some extra speakers. How about that one on the counter there?"

"Let me give you a demo of the radio," said Blackwater, ignoring Agent J's words. "Remarkable sound quality."

He twisted a dial.

Suddenly, the shop was filled with a weird, pulsating sound. It was high-pitched and wavering, like the scream of some sort of hideous monster. Agent J winced and screwed up his eyes, unable to stop the throbbing noise slicing through his thoughts.

Even the robots' sensors were partially affected by the intense sound waves. They shuddered and flinched, feeling shaken and dizzy.

Henry Blackwater watched Agent J impassively. The noise-cancelling headphones kept him shielded from the sonic vibrations that reverberated all around the shop.

Slowly, Agent J stood up straight. His face had become expressionless. His eyes were glazed and unfocused.

Blackwater switched off the radio. The pulsing sound died away. He removed his headphones and placed the radio back on the counter.

"How did you know my real name?" he said, staring angrily at Agent J.

"You were photographed," said Agent J flatly. "A few minutes ago. My HQ managed to ID you."

"Your HQ?" said Blackwater. "Where is your HQ?"

"In London."

"How did you find me?"

"Analysis of the circuits. Inside the speakers."

"What?" spluttered Blackwater. "That's not possible! How did you do it?"

"Not me. Other agents."

Inside the speaker, the robots' electronic brains had resisted the hypnotic effects of the sound. However, they were still readjusting their sensors and struggling to regain their normal functions.

"Agent J!" said Sabre, feeling slightly dazed. "He's under Blackwater's control!"

"He'll tell Blackwater about SWARM!" said Chopper.

CHAPTER SIX

"Call Sirena!" said Morph. "She's closest to them!"

"She doesn't have the weaponry needed to stop Blackwater," said Chopper.

"No, but I have!" said Sabre. "Nero, remove Widow's plug of webbing!"

With a swift punch from his pincer, Nero knocked out the web that Widow had spun to disguise the hole in the back of the speaker.

Meanwhile, Blackwater was still questioning Agent J. "Other agents?" he said, eyeing Agent J suspiciously. "What other agents? Who are you working for?"

CODE NAME FIRESTORM

Sabre buzzed across the counter. Staying low, so that Blackwater wouldn't spot him, he zipped across the shop then dived down towards floor level, his needle-like mouthparts whirring forward. A memory-blocking pellet was loaded up. He swooped at a small patch of sock, visible between Agent J's shoes and the hem of his trousers, and injected the pellet into Agent J's heel.

"Amnesia sting delivered," signalled Sabre.

Agent J flinched slightly. His eyes flickered.

"Logged," replied Chopper. "He hasn't worked with SWARM very long. That sting should remove his memory of us, and of SWARM HQ."

"Poor Agent J," said Morph, "he'll need to meet us for the first time, all over again."

"This is an emergency," said Chopper. "It had to be done."

Meanwhile, Blackwater was staring into Agent J's eyes. "Are you listening to me?"

"Blackwater has been wiping the memories of his victims," said Nero. "Now he'll get what humans call a taste of his own medicine."

Agent J's memory of SWARM had gone, but he was still under Blackwater's hypnotic influence.

"Yes. I'm listening."

"I asked who you're working for," said Blackwater.

Agent J seemed confused for a moment. Then he said "I work for MI5. I'm an MI5 agent."

Blackwater's face became a storm of fury and alarm. The robots were alarmed too.

"The sting's effect hasn't been strong enough!" said Sabre. "I'll deliver another!"

"No," said Chopper. "Those stings are designed to remove recent memories only. A second may cause permanent damage to Agent J's brain. It's too late, Blackwater knows that Agent J is part of the secret service. Agent J worked for MI5 for a long time before he was recruited by SWARM."

Blackwater took hold of the lapels of Agent J's jacket. "Say that again?" he whispered, through gritted teeth.

"I work for MI5," said Agent J.

"Who sent you here?" demanded Blackwater. "Which section chief?"

"I … I don't know," frowned Agent J. "I … work for MI5…"

"I've been betrayed," muttered Blackwater to

himself. "That low-down worm is trying to double-cross me!"

"Who does he mean?" said Morph.

"This confirms he's being helped from inside the secret service," said Chopper. "What's more, we now know he's being helped from inside MI5 itself!"

Outside in the street, Sirena was still positioned on the wall above the shop's window. "I'll transmit a full report to SWARM HQ," she said.

"Logged," said Chopper, inside the speaker.

Blackwater was pacing around the shop. His hands tapped together nervously. "Think, think, think," he said. "OK, they know about *this* place, but they don't know about *my* place."

He turned to face Agent J. "Confirm Firestorm Control, baseline alpha one."

"Confirmed," said the hypnotized Agent J.

"Go back to your HQ. Tell them you've investigated Trendi Soundz thoroughly. Tell them there's nothing suspicious here. They got it wrong."

"Nothing suspicious," said Agent J. "Confirmed."

"You'll forget you ever met me," said Blackwater.

"As far as you're concerned, this shop is run by … er, let's see … by a tall, curly haired woman called … Daisy Brown."

"Daisy Brown, confirmed," said Agent J.

"She offered you a cup of tea. She was very helpful. MI5 have got it all wrong about this shop."

"Very helpful," said Agent J. "Got it all wrong. Confirmed."

"Now go!"

Agent J turned and walked out of the shop. He headed across the street, then headed off in the direction of Tottenham Court Road.

"He doesn't even remember he drove here," said Sirena.

"You stay with Agent J," said Chopper. "Signal HQ to pick him up. We'll remain here, to keep track of Blackwater."

"Logged," said Sirena. She fluttered into the air, and followed Agent J down the street.

Blackwater stood in the window, watching Agent J walk away. "Let's hope that keeps them off my back for a while," he mumbled. "It won't work for long, though. Better hurry."

While Blackwater's back was turned, Sabre

returned to the speaker. He darted back through the hole Hercules had made and Widow immediately resealed it.

"Blackwater now thinks MI5 are closing in on him," said Nero. "His logical next move would be to speed up the Firestorm plan."

"We still don't know the full extent of that plan," said Chopper, "or what exactly he means by the word 'firestorm'."

Blackwater collected a large holdall from behind the counter. He bustled around the shop, dropping various tools and electronic equipment into it. He paused when he came to the speaker in which the SWARM robots were hiding. He hesitated, not sure whether to take it with him or not. In the end, he scooped it up and squashed it into the bag alongside everything else. "Might as well find out why this thing malfunctioned," he added.

He switched the sign on the door from "Open – Bargainz Inside" to "Closed – See Ya Laterz". He locked the front door of the shop from the inside, then pulled down a security grille inside the window and padlocked it.

Next he picked up his holdall and hurried behind the counter, through to the shop's small back room, which was piled high with stock and paperwork. Beyond that, past a heavily secured metal door, was a small car park. He dumped the holdall on the back seat of his large, rusty hatchback.

"Be careful," he mumbled. "Always be careful."

From his pocket, he pulled a device that resembled a calculator. He entered a short code into it. Inside the speaker, the robots' network was suddenly swamped by a fuzz of static. To counteract the effect, each insect fired a tiny, fibre-optic line to the robot next to them, forming a circle around which data could be rerouted.

"That's better," said Morph. "I don't like being out of touch. My sensors feel strange."

"That device of his is powerful enough to block all kinds of signals," said Nero. "Some of our sensor readings will experience interference, as well as our communications."

"Why is our recent upgrade to deal with signal jammers limited to fibre-optic lines?" said Morph. "Couldn't Professor Miller devise a way to overcome them entirely?"

"The only way to do that is to boost power output," said Nero. "We are very small. To generate enough energy, we'd have to carry around power cells the size of beach balls. It's simple physics. We have many advantages over humans but nobody's perfect. Blackwater must be worried about the possibility of being tracked or monitored."

"He's extremely cautious," said Morph.

"Hercules would make a joke about him being bugged," said Sabre. The stag beetle beside him remained dark and silent, burnt out and lifeless.

"This means we'll be out of range of HQ until he turns it off," said Chopper. "However, we must all remain in place here. Preventing Blackwater from carrying out any further attacks must be our first priority."

"I'll continue to cut Hercules free," said Nero.

The robots could feel that the car was now in motion, although Blackwater's signal blocker stopped their sensors keeping track of exactly where they were, and where they were going.

"At least we know why he added the extra

circuits into these speakers," said Sabre.

"He sold them to unsuspecting, and otherwise unconnected, members of the public," said Chopper. "The speakers would remain in his customers' homes, operating normally, until he activated the hypnotic wave circuits built into them. Then, those customers would become his servants."

"He must have relayed detailed verbal instructions to each victim through the speakers too," said Sabre. "He'll have told them where to collect all those gadgets, and how to operate them."

"The victims wouldn't even remember hearing the hypnotic signal," said Chopper. "Blackwater will have ordered them to forget it. If any of the attacks were foiled, as we foiled the first one, then he would remain undetected, in the background."

"It's a clever way of committing crimes by remote control," said Sabre. "Blackwater is clearly a genius at electronics."

"Although," said Nero, snipping at the circuit board around Hercules, "he hasn't been clever enough to outwit us."

Blackwater's car drove on through the streets of central London. By now, it was late afternoon. Darkness was creeping across the city.

5:42 p.m.

"Agent K is picking up Agent J and Sirena now," said Alfred Berners. He tapped at a large screen in the SWARM laboratory. "Poor Agent J's going to have a very confusing couple of hours!"

"We'll have to worry about that later," said Queen Bee. "Is Blackwater's signal blocker still operating?"

"Yes, at full power," said Alfred. "We've no way of knowing where the rest of the SWARM are until either it's turned off, or one of the robots can get far enough away from it."

"We can trust them to act correctly," said Queen Bee. "In the meantime, is there any way we can track Blackwater's movements from here?"

"I'm afraid not, Ms Maynard," said Alfred. "We don't know precisely what to look for. We don't

know if he's walking, or in the Underground, or in a car. The robots couldn't ID any vehicle or method of transport before they were cut off."

Simon Turing appeared, hurrying across the lab to intercept Queen Bee. "Agent K reports that the home address listed for Henry Blackwater is a dud. He lived there until about six months ago, but he's not there now, and his current address is unknown."

"Have you been able to mine more background data on him?" said Queen Bee.

"I have," said Simon. He called up information on the tablet he was carrying. "Henry Blackwater, forty-nine years old, born in England but spent most of his childhood in the Far East. His parents were both British electrical engineers, employed by a big international company. When Blackwater was twelve, terrorists tried to take over the area they were living in. Sixty people, including Blackwater's family, were held hostage for five weeks. MI6 agents, along with security forces from other countries, stormed the terrorists' compound. The raid was a total mess. The terrorists killed most of the hostages, including

Blackwater's parents and his two brothers.

"Henry was one of only three survivors. As you can imagine, as he grew up his attitude towards the terrorists who'd killed his family, and towards the secret services who'd bungled their rescue, wasn't exactly positive. He was a 'troubled' young man, who got involved with various political extremist groups. Despite that, his talents for electronics, chemistry and engineering were astounding. He was judged to have a glittering career in technology ahead of him.

"However, instead of that, he applied – believe it or not – to join both MI5 and MI6, as well as the CIA in America and several more security services across Europe. All of them turned him down. He was reckoned to be unstable and potentially violent. The interview panel at MI5 believed that he was only making these applications so that he could 'destroy the system from within'. Psychological assessment at the time said he was suspicious of others and hostile to authority. And also that he talked to himself a lot. For many years he scratched a living mending phones and computers. A few months ago, he seemed to vanish completely, then turned up running Trendi Soundz. Because of his background in revolutionary politics, MI5 have had him on their watch list for almost thirty years."

"What a strange and unhappy life," said Alfred Berners sadly. "But if MI5 are supposed to have him on their watch list, how come they don't know his current address?"

"I think we can put that down to Blackwater's MI5 contact," said Queen Bee. "It appears we've found another official record that's been deliberately deleted."

"And until the SWARM robots can give us a fix on him, he's out there on the loose somewhere," said Simon Turing. "I wonder what's made him start up this whole Firestorm business? Do you think it's something he's been planning for a long time?"

"Probably not," said Queen Bee. "Even people like Blackwater don't suddenly turn into big-time criminals at the drop of a hat. My guess is that his contact inside MI5 provided him with a few ideas about how he could cause chaos and gave him enough money to get started, and he's taken it from there."

"Why on earth would someone inside MI5 be helping him?" said Simon.

"That's something we still have to discover," said Queen Bee. "Blackwater is angry with the world and resentful over everything that's happened to him. The data he stole from MI6 will get him all the revenge he could desire."

"It's frightening," said Alfred in a low voice. "One person's tragedy could end up destroying us all."

"The international situation is getting worse by the hour," said Queen Bee. "Until the data is recovered, governments worldwide are ready to take drastic action to protect whatever secrets and secret agents might be at risk."

"And meanwhile, the public are wondering who or what Firestorm is, and demanding answers they can't be given," said Simon.

"I think we can now be pretty sure what those messages Blackwater left mean," said Queen Bee. "His motives and intentions are clear. His 'Firestorm' is nothing less than World War III."

6:07 p.m.

"Is that you, Henry?"

"Yes, Auntie Madge," called Blackwater irritably. Under his breath he added, "Who else would it be, you twit!"

The front door of Auntie Madge's house was old, worn and grubby, with paint peeling at its corners. The rest of the house looked much the same. Blackwater, carrying his holdall, bumped the door shut and shuffled through the hall and into the kitchen.

"I'm putting the tea on in a minute," called Auntie Madge from the living room.

"OK," called Blackwater.

"It's sausage and mash."

"OK."

He went out into the back garden. Tufts of weeds grew out of the cracks in the paving slabs. A saggy washing line had a selection of shirts and underpants pegged on it.

A large garage stood at the end of the yard, facing out onto a narrow alleyway that ran along the backs of the houses. Blackwater placed his hand onto a palm-print reader hidden inside an old wooden box fixed to the rear wall of the garage. There was a clanking sound from inside, as bolts were automatically drawn. Beside the box, a heavily reinforced metal door slid back. Blackwater glanced around to check that nobody was watching him, then entered the garage.

The metal entrance slid shut behind him with a clang. He touched a sensor, and the interior of the garage lit up brightly. It looked like a home-made version of SWARM's lab, packed with technology, screens and equipment.

He heaved his holdall up onto a table. He unzipped it and lifted out the speaker in which the SWARM robots were hiding. Then he rummaged in his pocket and switched off his signal jammer.

"Network back online," said Chopper. "Sensors at maximum."

"Our systems have returned to full function within this room," said Nero, "but the garage itself must be shielded. We still can't link to HQ."

"Let's take a detailed sensor sweep of this place," said Chopper.

Blackwater snatched up a phone that was

connected to a PC by a thick cable. His face was awash with anger. He tapped out a number from memory.

"Who's he calling?" said Morph.

"The line is hardwired to that handset," said Nero. "Without a physical connection to it, we can't tap it directly, so we can't hear who he's speaking to. However, I may be able to remotely break into Blackwater's phone system. I can try to back-trace the call, by using a wireless probe on that PC and tapping the public exchange."

"Proceed," said Chopper.

"Logged," said Nero. "It will take approximately 64.7 seconds."

"C'mon, c'mon," muttered Blackwater impatiently. His call was finally answered. For the moment, all that the robots could detect from the other end of the line was a faint echo of what Blackwater could hear through his phone.

"You've double-crossed me!" yelled Blackwater. "I've just had one of your lot turn up at the shop! … Yes, MI5! … Of course, I'm not kidding! … I don't care whether you authorized anything or not, an agent from MI5 was standing in my shop less than an hour ago... What? ... No, I used my hypnotic control on him, it doesn't allow subjects to lie!"

"Thirty-four seconds to an ID," said Nero.

"Yes, of course I dealt with it! He's gone away with his head full of rubbish," continued Blackwater. "But it was an emergency measure! If your lot are already sniffing around the shop, then how long before— Oh! You think you've guessed where this person might have come from after all, do you? ... What? ... Top-secret section? Which top-secret section? ... Oh, you don't know what they're called? Or the name of the woman who runs it? How convenient! In the meantime, I'm being tracked down by these people!"

"Nineteen seconds," said Nero.

"That's all very well for you to say! How do I know you're not lying to me? How do I know you're not setting me up? ... Yes ... Yes, I know you've given me equipment and information, but that proves nothing, does it? What? ... You've got everything to lose too, if things go wrong?"

"Seven seconds," said Nero.

"And that's a good enough reason why I

should keep trusting you, is it? Huh? … Well, that all sounds a bit hollow from where I'm standing, doesn't it?"

There was a click and a crackle on the robots' communications network. Nero's remote phone tap was online.

"Just calm down!" said the voice at the other end of Blackwater's call. It sounded warped and echoing on the robots' network, but already they were running a voice-print test. "I'm working on it, OK? I'll get them off our back, don't you worry."

"You'd better!" said Blackwater. "And while you're doing that, I'm bringing the timetable forward. Firestorm begins tonight!"

"No," said the voice. "Stay calm, and stick to the plan. Where are you, at the garage?"

"I'm not revealing my location over the phone!"

"All right, all right, Mr Paranoid. Just do as I say, right? Stay put and do nothing until I tell you. Stick to what we've agreed."

"Why should I?" cried Blackwater.

"Because if you don't, all our plans will be wasted, that's why. I'll sort this, OK?"

A high-pitched, three-note tone sounded over

the robots' network. "ID is confirmed," said Nero.

"Call me back when you've got better news," spat Blackwater. He stabbed angrily at the phone and the line went dead.

"Contact identified as MI5 agent Morris Drake," said Nero. "He is the one working with Blackwater from inside the secret service!"

6:12 p.m.

Queen Bee entered her office at SWARM HQ. Without bothering to sit down, she leaned across her desk and tapped at her screen.

"Sirena, report."

In the SWARM lab, Sirena the butterfly was logged into the computer system. "No contact with the other micro-robots yet, Queen Bee," she said. "I've been cross-referencing information downloaded from a number of databases. Since Blackwater's shop is in central London, we can safely assume that his base of operations, or at least his current home, is within commuting distance."

"Yes, that's likely," said Queen Bee.

"So, I've been working out where he went after he vanished from his last-known address. I've analyzed all records of housing across the entire city and checked those records against any possible link to Blackwater. Even if he used a fake ID, renting or buying a property would expose him to the risk of being tracked down. We know he's extremely cautious and paranoid about that sort of thing. His most logical course of action would have been to conceal himself in the home of a friend or family member."

"I can't believe he's got many friends," said Queen Bee.

"I've traced none," said Sirena. "But I have managed to track down an aunt of his, who lives in London. Her name is Margery Harris."

"Good work," said Queen Bee. "Get out there and check on this aunt, immediately. Given the speed at which Firestorm has acted so far, we haven't a moment to lose. Also, I'm worried about Agent Drake. We know he wants to take control of this operation. It's not like him to call me, as he did earlier, and then go silent. He's plotting something, I can feel it in my bones! Time could be running out for us, in more ways than one."

"Logged, Queen Bee. I'm on my way."

6:14 p.m.

At MI5, Agent Drake was holding a video conference with the prime minister and the home secretary. Two large computer screens were positioned on his desk. Both the politicians looked nervous and angry.

"You're certain about this, Drake?" said the home secretary.

"I am, ma'am," said Drake. "While the secret SIA section that's currently handling the Firestorm case has been... Well, we don't know what they've doing, do we? While they've been busy, I've had my own staff making enquiries, and we've made a breakthrough. A suspect had been identified, and tracked to an address in London, owned by a relative of his. An aunt, I believe."

"Where did this information come from?" said the prime minister.

Drake smiled to himself. "For the moment, sir, that must remain confidential. But the intel is good. I'd like permission to override … whatever this secret SIA section is called, and launch a full-scale raid on the address in question."

The home secretary turned to the prime minister on the other screen. "It's your call, Prime Minister."

"Why haven't the SIA come to us with this?" asked the prime minister. He turned to Drake. "More to the point, why didn't you take this to the section heading up the investigation?"

"Forgive me, sir," said Drake smoothly, "but officially I don't even know they exist, do I? Time is a factor here. Far quicker to come directly to you than to waste hours arguing about who should do what and when. We have to act fast."

The prime minister shifted nervously in his seat. "Yes, I see. You're sure of your facts? This raid will end the Firestorm threat?"

"I am absolutely certain of it, sir," smiled Drake.

"Very well," said the prime minister, "this

Firestorm business is an emergency. The world is looking to us for results. We'll sort out the protocols later. Get it done."

"Yes, sir," grinned Drake.

"Right, you have your orders, Mr Drake," said the prime minister. "Carry them out."

"Yes, sir."

6:20 p.m.

"Interesting," said Nero. "Detailed sensor sweeps of this garage reveal that Blackwater has got hold of some classified MI5 equipment. Drake must have given him a number of gadgets, which he's adapted, added to and built upon. He's created his own, more advanced, devices out of existing technology."

"I think the phrase Agent J used earlier today applies here," said Morph. "Curiouser and curiouser."

The robots were still safely hidden inside the speaker. Nero had now managed to cut Hercules free of the circuit he'd been fused to. The broken stag beetle lay on his side, his legs curled up beneath his body.

Henry Blackwater was clattering around the garage, loading gadgets, papers and tools into a large metal trunk. As usual, he was muttering endlessly to himself.

"He doesn't trust Agent Drake," said Nero. "He suspects that Drake may betray him to the authorities."

"We know for ourselves that Drake isn't trustworthy," said Chopper.

"Blackwater is probably preparing to put his Firestorm plan into effect, no matter what Drake says," said Nero.

"Right, stuff packed…" muttered Blackwater to himself. "Now then, let's see what happened to this speaker."

"Alert," said Chopper. "Blackwater will find us as soon as he opens up the back of the speaker. Sabre, prepare a memory sting. He must not be allowed to discover that we're robots."

"Logged," said Sabre calmly. "Flight path calculated. I'll fly out as soon as there's a gap wide enough for me. When his recent memory has been wiped, I'll also inject a freezer sting. Then he'll be immobilized."

"The Firestorm plot will be at an end," said Nero.

"All we'll need to do is get out of this garage and contact HQ," said Morph. "Blackwater will be captured, and we've gathered enough evidence to have Drake arrested."

"Get ready," said Chopper.

Blackwater sat on a tall stool in front of the table. He pulled the speaker and a set of screwdrivers closer to him. Then he reached across and grabbed a long pair of thick black rubber gloves. He pressed a sequence of keys on his PC.

Suddenly, there was a hum of power. A shimmering transparent dome slowly appeared over the speaker.

"It's a containment field," said Chopper, "very similar to the one used in the SWARM laboratory, when that briefcase was opened this morning."

"Then we're trapped," said Morph. "Sabre won't be able to get out to deliver a sting. We're going to be discovered!"

Blackwater's rubber gloves were held in mid-air by the force field. He could easily reach inside the barrier and work on the speaker, but nothing could get out. He flexed his fingers inside the gloves, then picked up a screwdriver and began to remove the speaker's rear panel.

"Does anyone have a brilliant idea at this point?" said Nero.

None of the other robots answered.

The back of the speaker lifted off. Blackwater set it down on the table and peered inside the speaker.

The SWARM robots stared back at him.

"Well, well," he said, his eyebrows rising in surprise. "What have we here?"

CHAPTER SEVEN

For a few seconds, Blackwater was fooled into thinking that the speaker was simply filled with actual insects. He sat back, puzzled, wondering if the speaker had been damaged by some sort of strange infestation.

"No, no..." he muttered. "That's a scorpion! And a dragonfly... What on earth?"

He leaned closer again and poked at the robots with the end of his screwdriver. Their electronic eyes stared back at him.

"Perhaps if I fly at full speed," said Sabre, "I can break through the energy barrier?"

"Negative," said Nero. "Sensors show it's almost as powerful as the one at HQ. You'd only bounce off it!"

To Blackwater, the insects remained still and silent. He prodded at Nero with the screwdriver. "I don't believe it," he gasped. "Mechanical! This must be what Drake was on about…"

The expression on his face slowly turned from amazement to fury. He hopped off the stool and backed away.

"This proves it!" he cried. "That scumbag has double-crossed me. 'Stay put and do nothing until I tell you,' he said. Meanwhile, they're closing in on me! Well, he can forget our agreement… Firestorm is all mine now!" He chuckled to himself. "I was going to turn him in anyway, sooner or later. Right, first things first… I need to buy myself a little time."

He crossed over to his PC and searched through the hard drive for a preprepared video file, then set it to upload.

"Isn't there anything we can do?" said Morph.

"For the moment, no," said Chopper. "Our cover is blown."

Blackwater returned to the force field. He slipped a hand back into one of the gloves and picked up the screwdriver again. With the other hand, he slid a tall, bulbous machine across the table, until it loomed over the force field and the speaker inside.

At one end of the machine was a long tube. It was attached to the main part of the machine by a set of hinged rods, rather like an office desk lamp. Blackwater twisted the arm around so that the tube pointed directly down at Hercules.

A large magnifying glass, on a long flexible metal arm, was pulled across the desk too. One of Blackwater's piercing blue eyes suddenly loomed over the robots, huge and glassy. He prodded the damaged stag beetle with his screwdriver.

"Very sophisticated little robots, these," he mumbled. "No wonder they're kept secret. Not sure even I could make something similar. Hmm, good thing they're sealed off in here, I bet they're just packed with communications devices…"

He poked at Nero and Chopper. "Eh?" he said, raising his voice. He talked to them as if he was a small boy talking to a helpless mouse he'd caught in a trap. "I'd love to pull you all apart, bit by bit, to see what makes you tick. But I haven't got time right now, and I daren't try to keep you or you'll be buzzing off the minute you get the chance, telling the world where I am. I knew keeping that signal jammer with me at all times was a wise move, you'll all have been out of touch with your base for ages, thank goodness. Thought I'd be jamming bugs of a different kind, though, eh?"

He grinned at them. His features looked weird and distorted through the magnifying glass.

"I bet you've got some nasty little weapons, too, hmm? Scorpion, dragonfly, spider, centipede, mosquito… And this broken one's a beetle. Looks like he interfered with my circuits, and they zapped him right back. Still, we'll soon have him put to rights."

Blackwater switched on the machine. Parts of the tube began to glow in sequence. A sharp, bright beam of blue light shot down through the energy barrier and engulfed Hercules.

Slowly, his legs began to straighten. Power pulsed through his circuits. His systems began to run through a rapid self-repair cycle.

"What's happening to him?" said Morph.

"I detect energized particles inside that light beam," said Nero. "They're triggering his circuits to break down and then redirect the molecules in his mechanics. In short, he's being repaired."

"Not even Professor Miller at SWARM's lab can do that!" said Sabre.

Suddenly, the robots heard a crackle on their communications network. It was Hercules.

"R... R... Reboot..."

6:40 p.m.

"Ms Maynard, you've got to see this!" cried Simon Turing.

In the laboratory at SWARM HQ, Queen Bee turned towards the large screen on the wall. Simon clicked a link on his tablet. The display showed an online video-sharing site.

"This was uploaded to GoggleVox a few minutes ago," said Simon. "It's Firestorm."

The video began to play. A silhouetted figure

sat in front of a moving image of the Earth revolving inside a ball of flame. A slow drumbeat and the sound of a howling wind played in the background.

A series of names began to scroll up the left-hand side of the screen. Underneath each name were brief descriptions of top-secret spying operations carried out in the past three years.

The silhouetted figure spoke. His voice has been heavily disguised and it came out as a deep, terrifying growl.

"Governments of the world, please listen carefully. The names you can see are MI6 agents operating in Western Europe. You know what was taken from MI6 headquarters in London. You know this is real. You also know that this is just a tiny sample of the data I possess. These names will cause severe embarrassment for the UK government. They reveal who Britain has been using to spy on her friends in Europe. Think how much worse it'll be when I reveal the names and activities of every MI6 agent in China. Or every spy mission carried out by the West in North Korea."

Professor Miller and Alfred Berners came to stand beside Simon Turing and Queen Bee. All of them stared in horror at the screen.

"If any move is made against me," continued the voice, "all the data will be released. If any attempt is made to take down this video, the data will *all* be released. If MI6, or anyone else, tries to silence me, the data will all be released. I hope that's clear. The Firestorm is here! The countdown to your destruction has begun!"

6:45 p.m.

Blackwater dragged the trunk he'd filled across the floor of the garage. He paused to tap a series of commands into his PC. From inside the speaker, none of the SWARM robots could see what he was doing. The final command read:

```
Robot reprogramming =>
full destruction subroutine inserted
```

Then he looked over his shoulder at the table. The repair beam was still shining brightly into the domed energy barrier, busily fixing Hercules.

"Pity," he said to the robots trapped inside the speaker. "I wish I could have kept you." He looked around at all the equipment in the garage. "And I wish I could have kept more of this too. Still, there's only so much room in one car, I guess."

"What exactly has he got in that trunk?" said Morph.

"Scans would suggest some kind of basic survival kit," said Chopper. "There's a small but powerful electrical generator, compressed food rations, clothing, some kitchen equipment and other essentials. There's also a large collection of his gadgets and weapons, plus computers. He's carrying all the data that was stolen from MI6, and all the money stolen earlier on."

Blackwater dragged the trunk from the garage and out of sight. Meanwhile, the beam that was focused on Hercules appeared to have almost finished doing its job. The micro-robot stag beetle's toughened exoskeleton was looking as shiny as new, and his razor-sharp claw was beginning to twitch with life.

"Rebooting," he said. "Full systems check… Online."

"His voice sounds slightly different," said Morph. "I wonder why?"

Outside the garage, Blackwater was dragging the trunk across the courtyard towards the house. He didn't take any notice of the butterfly that was fluttering high above his head. Grunting with effort, he heaved the trunk over the back step into the kitchen.

Flying above the garage, Sirena signalled to SWARM headquarters. "Hive 2 to HQ, Blackwater's presence at this address is confirmed. He appears to have assembled a survival kit. It looks like he's preparing to leave for good."

"Any contact with the rest of the SWARM?" asked Simon.

"Negative," said Sirena, "but the garage at the rear of the house is heavily shielded. Power drainage scans show it's soaking up a lot of electricity. That's almost certainly his base of operations, and where the other robots are."

"An ordinary garage?" said Simon.

"Should I try to find a way in?" asked Sirena. "The others may need help."

"Queen Bee's orders are to stay close to Blackwater," said Simon. "If you get the chance, then—"

"Wait," interrupted Sirena. "Long-range sensors are picking up a lot of movement… Approaching from the north, west and south-east."

"That's quite a densely populated street," said Simon. "Are you sure you're not just picking up local residents?"

"Negative," said Sirena. "Movement patterns indicate stealth and coordination. They're still seventy-five metres from Blackwater's house, but closing in slowly." She flew up slightly, allowing her highly sensitive antennae to detect every possible piece of data. "They are heavily armed, and wearing bulletproof jackets. Weaponry, uniform type and tactics indicate an MI5 assault squad."

"Drake!" said Simon. "If he rushes in now, he'll ruin everything. If Blackwater sees those agents and panics, he'll almost certainly release that stolen data onto the internet!"

"Reboot complete," announced Hercules.

"Welcome back," said Nero. "I'm picking up some odd power fluctuations in your circuits. Are you functioning correctly?"

Hercules scuttled towards the other robots. His wing case slowly opened, and his large, powerful wings unfolded. Suddenly, lights appeared in his eye cameras. Red ones.

"Functioning correctly," he said flatly. "Reprogramming successful. Full destruction subroutine acknowledged. I must obey. Destruction of micro-robots commencing."

CHAPTER EIGHT

6:49 p.m.

"Your tea's getting cold!" cried Auntie Madge. "I told you not to be long. I wish I knew what you got up to in my garage, all hours of the day and night."

"I told you, Auntie Madge, it's a special project," said Blackwater. "Don't be so nosy."

"Don't you be so rude, young man!" said Auntie Madge.

"Sorry, Auntie," smiled Blackwater.

It was dark outside. The dull glow of street

lights shone through the living-room window.

Blackwater opened his heavy trunk and took out a pair of headphones. He put them on and walked over to the portable radio that was perched on the windowsill close to his aunt's chair.

"Want the radio on, Auntie Madge?"

"What? No, thanks."

"I'll put it on anyway," said Blackwater.

He pressed the radio's power button. At the same time, he pressed a button on a small remote control he had in his pocket. Instantly, the radio began to emit a loud, pulsing sound. The extra circuit he'd built into it was identical to the ones found in the speakers at Trendi Soundz. The sound rippled across the room, in waves of noise so intense they were almost visible.

For a moment, Auntie Madge sat in her armchair with a look of bewilderment on her face. Then her eyes glazed over, becoming distant and unfocused.

Blackwater switched off the radio. The hypnotic signal cut out and he replaced the headphones in his trunk.

"Confirm Firestorm Control," he said.

Auntie Madge got up from her armchair and stood straight. "Control Code Name Firestorm is in place," she said in a flat voice.

"You will defend the house and the garage with your life," said Blackwater.

"With my life, confirmed."

"You will deploy weapons as I showed you last week, when I hypnotized you before."

"Deploy weapons, confirmed."

"You will attack anyone who tries to enter. You will show no mercy. You will remain hidden and allow any attackers to believe that it's me operating the weapons."

Auntie Madge's lips trembled slightly. "No … mercy… Confirmed."

Blackwater smiled to himself. "Right," he whispered. "I'm off. Goodbye, Auntie."

"Hercules is repaired, but he's also fully under Blackwater's control," said Nero.

Without warning, the stag beetle suddenly lunged at Chopper. His cutting claw clacked savagely at the dragonfly's wings. Chopper darted out of the way just in time.

"I'll try to break into Hercules's programming through our communications network," said Nero.

"Be quick!" said Morph. "We're trapped inside this force field with him!"

Widow leaped across the stag beetle's path and fired looping lengths of web around him. With lightning speed, Hercules spun in mid-air, slicing the cords of webbing apart with one edge of his claw.

Using Widow's attack as cover, Morph flung himself up and around Hercules. The centipede's gelatinous, flexible body quickly squeezed and tightened, pulling Hercules's wing case closed and forcing him to tumble over onto his back.

"Quick!" said Morph. "He's too powerful for me – he'll snap me in half! Someone find a way to disable his systems."

"I can't hack into his program," said Nero. "Blackwater's added too many firewalls."

"Sabre, Nero, will either of your stings take him offline?" said Chopper.

"Negative," said Sabre, "our weaponry won't work on machines, and especially not on robots like us."

Hercules powered up his exoskeleton. He was fitted with a variety of tools to help him tunnel through almost anything. He could even melt his way through metal.

"He's heating up!" said Morph. "My systems might overload!"

Chopper, Nero and Widow joined the battle. The robots grappled around the inside of the speaker. Nero was thrown back with a kick from two of the stag beetle's legs. Sabre had to whip from side to side to avoid being crushed in Hercules's claw. Morph, his components getting steadily hotter, held on tightly to restrict Hercules's movements as much as he could. Despite the beetle's superior strength, the others managed to keep him at bay, by working together.

"Combined attack may result in defeat," said Hercules. The red lights in his eyes flashed sharply. "Link to main computer now established."

Suddenly, the energy barrier above the robots vanished.

"We're free!" said Morph.

"He's connected himself to Blackwater's PC," said Sabre.

At that moment, all around the garage, machinery juddered and blinked into life. An array of Blackwater's weapons had switched themselves on.

"Oh no," said Morph quietly.

"Reprogramming must be obeyed. Full destruction subroutine must be obeyed," said Hercules. "Total destruction of robots and all garage contents. Begin."

At the far end of the garage, a barrage of miniature rockets launched.

"Hive 2 to HQ, I'm tracking Blackwater," signalled Sirena. "He's loaded that trunk in his car and he's driving away. I'm on the roof of the car."

"Stay with him," said Queen Bee, from the SWARM laboratory. "Where are Drake's assault squad?"

"They're getting close to the house," said

Sirena. "They haven't seen Blackwater leave. I've had no indication that he knows they're so close. He doesn't realize how narrowly he's avoided them."

"However, we can be sure he's prepared for whoever he thinks might come to get him, whether it's the police, MI5 or us," said Queen Bee. "We know he favours booby traps. That house is probably full of them!"

"Can't we have MI5's attack called off?" said Sirena. "They may end up hurt."

"I doubt Drake would listen, if it was *us* warning him," said Queen Bee.

At that moment, MI5 agent Drake raised a walkie-talkie to his lips. "Go! Go! Go!"

All the members of his squad broke into a run. They emerged into the open, charging towards the front of the house and down the alleyway that ran along behind the garage.

Inside the house, the hypnotized Auntie Madge could hear the thudding of boots.

She watched through the living-room window. She could see the dark flak jackets and helmets of the MI5 agents in the glow of the street lights. Their machine guns glinted.

She picked up the remote control for her TV. Blackwater had made a number of hidden modifications to its circuits. She pressed a long sequence of buttons.

Up in the dusty attic, where Blackwater had told Auntie Madge he was storing some stock from the shop, a series of lights flashed. Hatches sprung open on the outside of the roof.

Below, one of the MI5 agents slapped Drake on the shoulder. "Sir! Up there! Something coming at us!"

"What?" said Drake.

A rain of small explosive spheres suddenly fell all around them. Each one detonated as it hit the ground. The agents were knocked back as fireballs burst into the air with a series of thunderous bangs. The same thing was happening to the agents approaching the house from other directions.

Machinery in the attic sent a second wave

shooting out of the hatches in the roof. This time, sticky, football-sized blobs of Blackwater's instant-setting sealant were rapidly fired out. They emitted low bleeps, as heat-seeking electronics inside guided them at speed towards anyone nearby. Any MI5 agent who couldn't dodge them quickly enough found themselves glued to the ground by an arm or a leg.

"Blackwater's not giving up without a fight!" Drake yelled into his walkie-talkie. "All units, prepare to move in on my signal!"

Inside the garage, everything was ablaze. The miniature rockets, fired at Hercules's command, had exploded in sheets of flame.

The SWARM robots faced three dangers at once: attack from Hercules's razor-sharp claw, the spreading fire, and the weaponry that was activating all around them. Like the MI5 agents outside, the robots found themselves targeted by all kinds of Blackwater gadgets and booby traps.

The insects darted in every direction, spreading

out across the garage. All were desperately trying to stay out of reach of one deadly attack or another.

"When Hercules said 'total destruction' he wasn't kidding!" said Morph, squeezing under Blackwater's PC to avoid the flames.

"Blackwater must be determined to leave no evidence," said Chopper. He zipped around, avoiding a stream of electrical darts, his brain calculating flight paths a billion times a second.

"There's no way to escape this garage," said Morph. "Everything is sealed and shielded. The door is too tightly fixed for even me to squeeze under."

"Is there no way to deal with Hercules?" said Sabre. He was flying at top speed, staying only a few centimetres ahead of the stag beetle's snapping claw. "If his link to Blackwater's computers can be broken, perhaps we can stop all this destruction?"

"I have an idea," said Nero. "The risk of severe damage is high, but if it works it'll restore Hercules to normal. Sabre, direct him this way."

"Logged," said Sabre. He dived down,

swooping over Nero, who was scuttling across the table. As Hercules flashed past in pursuit, Nero hooked his tail around Hercules and was whipped up into the air.

The stag beetle twisted, ready to hurl Nero aside. From the scorpion's back, a fibre-optic probe darted out and sunk itself into Hercules's head. The probe was normally used to hack computers. What it might do when connected to another robot, not even Nero could guess.

"Power surge!" cried Nero. "Sensors overloading! Will … try to … hack Hercules's reprogramming…"

Suddenly, Hercules's power systems shut down. The stag beetle dropped to the floor like a pebble, taking Nero with him.

Meanwhile, the fire in the garage was raging. The temperature rising rapidly. Blackwater's weaponry had started to misfire and malfunction, sending explosive charges and crackling electrical arcs spinning everywhere.

"There's no way we can stop it!" cried Morph.

"Mission priority is to escape," said Chopper.

"But how?" asked Morph.

"By making things worse," said Chopper. "Morph, you're beneath Blackwater's computer. Insert a destruct command into every weapon in the system at once."

"But that will cause an explosion," said Morph. "Even Blackwater didn't intend that! He only wanted to gut the inside of this place. Anything visible from outside would draw attention."

"There's no alternative now," said Chopper. "Don't worry, we're tough enough to survive the blast. In theory, at least."

"Logged," said Morph. He quickly squeezed over to the thick cable that joined Blackwater's computer to the rest of the equipment in the garage. He stabbed into the cable with his antennae to establish a live connection into the data stream. "I hope this doesn't damage us too badly."

He sent the command.

CHAPTER NINE

Less than a second later, the whole garage shuddered and rocked. An explosive force cracked the walls and punched a wide split in the ceiling. The door trembled, then fell off and dropped forward with a loud clang.

At their positions outside the house, the MI5 agents flinched and looked at each other. Drake barked into his walkie-talkie. "Looks like Blackwater's chucking bombs at us now! But he won't get away! Move in – full force."

The inside of the garage was a smoking, blackened ruin. Every last item of Blackwater's equipment was either burnt or completely destroyed.

For a moment, in the dark courtyard, there was silence. Then the SWARM robots shot out through the open doorway. Chopper carried Morph, while Widow spun her way along micro-threads. Sabre was followed by Hercules, who held Nero in his folded legs. All the robots were singed and grimy, but still fully functioning. Chopper immediately transmitted a package of data back to HQ, including the information that Drake had been working with Blackwater.

"Remarkably little damage," said Sabre. "To us, I mean."

"Hercules?" said Chopper.

"Nero's cure worked," said the stag beetle. "Blackwater's subroutine has been deleted from my programming."

"My sensors need to be realigned," said Nero, "but I'm unharmed."

Sabre buzzed in a way which a human might have said was grumpy.

Queen Bee cut into the robots' communication network. "Good to hear from you all," she said, "but there's no time to spare. Get out of there right now."

As she spoke, Drake and his MI5 agents kicked in the front door of the house. The robots could hear shouts, and their X-ray sensors picked up agents charging through every room. Auntie Madge stood calmly, still under the influence of her nephew's hypnotic signal.

The robots flew up and over the house, heading away at top speed.

"We've received your info on Agent Drake," said Queen Bee. "You can leave him to us. Let him and his men go running round that house for a while, it'll keep them out of our way. Sirena is on the roof of Blackwater's car. Home in on her signal. We don't know where he's going, but that car has to be stopped."

"He's got the stolen MI6 data with him," said Chopper.

"Exactly," said Queen Bee. "And he knows about you now, which makes it all the more important that he doesn't realize you're after him. He's almost certainly got some gadget rigged up to release the data online if he even suspects he's cornered. Get him, and get that data. Otherwise half the world could be at war by morning!"

"We're live, Queen Bee," replied the robots.

7:04 p.m.

At SWARM HQ, Queen Bee and Simon Turing were watching screens showing each robot's visual and sensor data. Images of everything the robots were seeing were overlaid with flowing streams of information.

"What's the situation since the release of that video?" said Queen Bee.

"Major news stories across the world," said Simon. "A lot of arguments between diplomats and politicians. The foreign secretary is flying to Brussels as we speak to hold talks with the governments of EU countries. Social media are going mad. People in various countries are demanding to know what's going on. It's being contained, but if more data gets out, we're in big trouble. Blackwater was very clever. He released

just enough secrets to start a few rows, nothing more. For now."

"At least we can get that traitor Drake out of the picture once and for all," said Queen Bee. "I'm due to take a conference call with the PM and the home secretary in –" she checked her watch – "four minutes. Drake can expect to be arrested within the hour."

"Let's hope the robots can deal with Blackwater," said Simon.

"Yes," said Queen Bee quietly. "They're our only hope right now."

7:09 p.m.

Blackwater's rusty white car sped along, surrounded by the lights of the city. He was driving out of London, heading west.

"You need to hurry," signalled Sirena. "He's stopping and starting now, because of the traffic, but he'll get to the motorway in approximately ninety seconds. Once he's at full speed, he'll be moving too fast for you to catch up."

"Logged," said Chopper. "We're less than five hundred metres away now. Closing in."

"Is the car itself booby-trapped?" said Nero.

"Possibly," said Sirena. "We should proceed with care. Scans show the rear of the vehicle contains only the luggage, plus some bags containing more clothes and electronic spare parts. However, I'm reading some odd electrical activity behind the car's dashboard. He's made modifications, but what they are I can't be sure."

"Logged," said Chopper. "Where's the data?"

"The USB stick containing the stolen MI6 data is inside the case, linked up to a laptop and a transmitter."

"Has he made duplicates of the data?"

"I've searched all the computer memory in the luggage. There are laptop hard drives, solid-state memory cards and other USB sticks. None show data patterns similar to the USB stick with the data on it. That would seem to be the only copy. I'm sending you an exact fix on it now."

"Received," said Chopper. "Four hundred metres and closing. "

"What's the best way to stop him?" said Morph. "A flat tyre?"

"I could sting a tyre and cause what would look like an accidental blow-out," said Sabre. Then he corrected himself: "No, I tried that on a moving car during the Operation Sting investigation. It didn't work."

"Perhaps we should get into the engine?" said Nero. "We could cause a mechanical fault, which would force him to stop?"

"Whatever we do," said Chopper, "we must remember Queen Bee's orders. He must not realize that it's us trying to stop him."

"Logged," replied the others.

Blackwater tapped the car's indicator. The long ramp to the motorway was coming up on his left. His fingers jittered nervously against the steering wheel.

Suddenly, he slapped his hand on the wheel. "Idiot! I've let my own thoughts distract me! Stupid! Stupid! Stupid!" He reached into his pocket and pulled out his signal jammer. With one hand, and keeping his eyes on the road, he entered the code to turn it on.

"Something's powering up," said Sirena. "I think it's—"

She vanished from the robots' network.

"Where's she gone?" said Morph.

Chopper's night vision zoomed in on the car ahead. Sirena was still on the roof, the microscopic grippers on her thin legs holding her firmly in place.

All the robots could now detect a strange blank spot in their sensor grid.

"He really is extremely cautious," said Morph.

"We're less than a hundred metres from the car," said Chopper. "If we get any closer, we'll lose communications ourselves."

"Our sensors will not function either, remember," said Nero. "Sirena said there may be more booby traps. We'll be going in blind. Our chances of success will fall dramatically."

"We have to act fast!" said Morph. "The car is heading up the ramp. It'll be on the motorway in a few seconds."

Nero made a lightning-quick scan of the area around them. "I have an alternative plan. Hercules, catch up with the car and deal with the stolen data. Beware of sensor malfunction."

"Logged," said Hercules. He shot off ahead.

"The rest of us will land on the roof of that articulated lorry parked outside the cafe on the other side of the road. Its steering and engine are controlled by a computer in the cab. We can hack into the computer and therefore control the lorry. We can chase Blackwater's car, and remain out of range of the signal jammer."

Up ahead, Blackwater manoeuvred the car out onto the motorway, which snaked away into the distance supported on massive concrete pillars. His headlights shone onto the stretch of road in front of him. The noise of the car's wheels against the tarmac rose to a dull roar as he accelerated. Although it was now early evening, there were relatively few vehicles either ahead of him, or behind him.

Meanwhile, an angry lorry driver came running out of the roadside cafe. He yelled helplessly as he watched the back end of his lorry driving away up the motorway ramp.

Ahead, Hercules adjusted his flight pattern and landed lightly on the rear window of Blackwater's car. His sensors felt dull and swamped, like a human feeling the effects of a heavy cold.

Tiny laser cutters clicked into place at the end of his claw. He rested them against the window and the claw began to rotate. Miniature laser beams sliced through the glass. Seconds later, a neatly cut circle dropped away, and Hercules climbed through into the car's interior.

"So far, so good," he added to his internal log.

Quickly, he crawled across to the large trunk. It sat on the folded-down rear seats, and took up most of the space in the back of the car. He paused to consult the data Sirena had sent over, about exactly where the stolen MI6 data was located. He scuttled a little to the right, then began to cut into the trunk with his claw.

Blackwater glanced into his rear-view mirror. The headlights of the lorry reflected into his eyes.

"Wretched lorry drivers," he muttered. "Driving too close. Come on, then, overtake me..."

The lorry maintained a steady speed, following exactly behind Blackwater's car. Inside the lorry's cab, Nero was at the windscreen, looking out at the road. Morph had squeezed himself behind

the touchscreen on the dashboard and hacked directly into the lorry's computer. He relayed data to the others. Chopper, Widow and Sabre were standing by.

"Increase speed by three per cent," said Nero. "Steering four point five degrees to the right." The vehicle's automated systems did exactly as he told them. The large steering wheel turned slightly, and the accelerator rose, as if operated by an invisible man.

"I wonder how Hercules is doing," said Morph. "Is Sirena OK?"

On the roof of the car, the butterfly made quick movements with her wings, signalling back to Nero. "She's fine," said Nero.

The massive supports beneath the motorway were slowly reducing in height, as the road left London behind. Soon it was at ground level, no longer raised above the streets. Instead, it cut through a wide valley, with steep grassy hills to each side. The lorry rumbled along behind Blackwater's car.

"Traffic density is light," said Chopper. "Let's move in on our target."

The lorry suddenly revved up. Its speed increased and its front bumper moved to within a few metres of Blackwater's car.

"We mustn't endanger human life!" said Morph.

"We are far more efficient at driving than any human," said Nero calmly. "The best way to safeguard human life is to get Blackwater off the road as fast as possible."

"Make sure we stay at a distance from the signal jammer," said Chopper.

"Logged," said Nero.

In his car, Blackwater kept glancing nervously at the headlights coming up behind him. "What's this fool doing? What's he *doing*?"

The lorry suddenly swerved to the right. With its engine roaring, it raced ahead and quickly drew level with the car. Blackwater watched in alarm as the lorry's huge wheels moved up alongside him.

"Widow," said Chopper calmly.

"I'm live," said Widow. She swung herself out of the lorry's cab. Leaping from lorry to car and back again, she spun a broad web between the two,

its threads thinner than a human hair but stronger than steel cable. Seconds later, once the car was firmly tethered to the lorry, she swung back into the cab again. "Web binding completed."

Blackwater hadn't spotted what Widow had done. All he knew was that as the lorry moved, so did his car. His rusty hatchback was no match for the enormous power of the lorry.

"Take him off the road," said Chopper.

Nero sent instructions into the lorry's computer. The vehicle began to drift to the left.

Blackwater was panicking. "Hey!" he screamed at the non-existent lorry driver. "You maniac! You're going to hit me if you're not careful! Oi!"

He pressed the car's brake pedal, but as he did so the car lurched violently. It was tied to the lorry so securely that the lorry simply dragged it along.

In the lorry's cab, Nero's millisecond-by-millisecond driving compensated for the drag of the car. The hatchback bumped and bashed against the side of the lorry. The signal jammer bounced off the seat beside Blackwater. It clattered around until it hit the gear stick and broke apart.

"What's going on?" screamed Blackwater. "Stop! Stop!"

Nero gradually guided the lorry off the motorway onto the hard shoulder, dragging the car along with it. Clouds of grit flew up around the wheels. The car scraped across the ground and one of its tyres burst with a deafening bang.

The lorry continued to steer left. It drove off the hard shoulder onto the grass beyond, rumbling over the bumpy surface. Blackwater's car did the same.

At last, the lorry came to a halt. The car, its right side badly dented, juddered until its engine cut out.

Blackwater leaned across the passenger seat and scrambled through the glove compartment. "Something's going on… This is *them*… They've tracked me down, somehow… Well, they'll be sorry! They'll be sorry!"

He found a smartphone he'd hidden underneath a stack of computer printouts. He sat up in his seat again, tapping gleefully at the phone, chuckling to himself.

He stopped mid-tap. The smile dropped

from his face. Perched on the car's steering wheel were a butterfly, a spider, a scorpion, a dragonfly, a mosquito and a centipede. The human and the robots gazed silently at each other for a moment.

"You?" gasped Blackwater. "How?" His smile returned. "You're too late!"

He raised the smartphone up in front of them. A large round button on its screen glowed red. "Now, all that data goes public. It uploads to the internet. It's bye bye, peace and harmony, and there's nothing you can do about it!"

He pressed the button. An error message appeared:

CONTACT BROKEN. DATA CANNOT BE FOUND.

He pressed the button again. And again. Then he bashed the smartphone against the steering wheel until it smashed into half a dozen pieces. He buried his face in his hands, and yelled angrily at the top of his voice.

Hercules appeared on the headrest beside Blackwater.

"The stolen data is completely wiped off the USB stick?" said Chopper.

"I bombarded it with magnetic radiation about two minutes ago," said Hercules. "Sirena's directions were perfect. I tunnelled in a direct line through two laptops, and there it was."

"You're welcome," said Sirena.

"Message sent to SWARM HQ," said Nero. "Agent K will be here to arrest Blackwater shortly."

"Sabre," said Chopper.

The mosquito buzzed in mid-air for a moment. Blackwater looked up, scowling with rage. He was just in time to see Sabre dart forward and inject a memory-wiping pellet into his neck.

Blackwater yelped, and slapped a hand to his neck. Sabre darted forward again, and injected a freezer sting into the other side. Blackwater yelped again, then toppled over sideways.

"He won't remember us at all," said Chopper. "SWARM remains secret."

CHAPTER TEN

The following day, in the laboratory at SWARM HQ, Queen Bee brought her team up to date. The robots were all in their metallic nests, raised above the workbench. The residue from the garage explosion had been cleaned off them, and they were recharging their power cells.

"Drake's safely under lock and key, then?" said Alfred Berners.

Queen Bee nodded. "And Blackwater too. MI6 have been able to assure the world that their data is secure again. Mind you, there are a number of governments who want to ask them some awkward questions, but I think we can leave that to them."

"Why did Drake do it?" said Simon Turing. "What was he hoping to gain?"

"He was ruthless and ambitious," said Queen Bee. "But he'd also, in the past, made errors and enemies. He'd even been made to look a fool by this department, don't forget. He wasn't exactly thought of as MI5's finest, but he badly wanted to get ahead. He wanted to get promoted to a better job, and above all he wanted to be thought of as a hero."

"So he cooked up a plot to make himself look good," said Simon.

"Exactly," said Queen Bee. "He found someone on MI5's watch list, someone with a grudge who might be turned into a terrorist."

"Blackwater," said Simon.

"Drake erased records to allow Blackwater to remain hidden, and supplied him with secret MI5 equipment, and information about MI6, in order to help him create a serious threat. He thought he could easily control Blackwater. He underestimated Blackwater's determination and his intelligence. Drake thought he could allow Blackwater to set his plan in motion, then sweep in and arrest him at the critical moment, before any major harm was done."

"So that he would look like the most brilliant secret-service agent ever, the genius who'd cracked the world-shattering Firestorm case," said Simon.

"Drake didn't really think Blackwater would get a chance to release that MI6 data," said Queen Bee. "He genuinely thought he could contain the situation. He was wrong. That's why he was so keen to take charge of the investigation. He thought he'd be given it automatically and never realized it might end up in our laps! He made some disastrous mistakes."

"Sad, really," said Alfred. "Blackwater's case is a sad one too."

"Yes, I think you're right," said Queen Bee. "It seems he was driving off to hide out in the countryside, for when the bombs started dropping. From some secret hideout in the middle of nowhere, he thought he could dangle the threat of World War III over the government.

Although, I can't imagine it would have been for long, can you?"

"It doesn't make sense," said Simon. "Did he seriously want to cause a war?"

"Sense was the last thing on his mind," shrugged Queen Bee. "He was raging against the world. I'm not sure he knew what he wanted himself, deep down."

"Well," said Professor Miller, "one thing we do know. Drake and Blackwater both underestimated each other."

"That's true," said Nero, from the workbench. "And they both underestimated SWARM too."

The interrogation room at MI5 was small and grey. A single dim light was set flat into the high ceiling. Ex-agent Morris Drake sat at a small table, leaning back in his chair, staring defiantly at the man opposite him. This man was tall and thin – a professional interrogator.

"There's no way out of this, Drake," he said softly. "Your only chance is to make a full

confession, and face the consequences."

"Prison?" grunted Drake. "Disgrace? No, I'll give that a miss."

"You can't. You know you can't."

Drake leaned forward. Shadows lengthened down his face. "Yes, I can. I know about certain … foreign projects. Things you're going to want to know about too."

The interrogator shifted uncomfortably. "What … things?"

"Things that are coming," said Drake in a whisper. "Dangerous things."

OUT MAY 2015

SIMON CHESHIRE

DEPARTMENT OF MICRO-ROBOTIC INTELLIGENCE

SWARM

TARGET SILVERCLAW

SIMON CHESHIRE

Simon is the award-winning author of the *Saxby Smart* and *Jeremy Brown* series. Simon's ultimate dream is to go the moon, but in the meantime, he lives in Warwick with his wife and children. He writes in a tiny room, not much bigger than a wardrobe, which is crammed with books, pieces of paper and empty chocolate bar wrappers. His hobbies include fixing old computers and wishing he had more hobbies.

www.simoncheshire.co.uk